ABIGAIL HORNSEA

Summer
of
Spies

A thoroughly modern
Belle Bright adventure

Summer of Spies

A Belle Bright Adventure

Copyright © 2013 by Abigail Hornsea

First published in Great Britain in 2013 by **Pepik Ltd**.
First published in the United States by **Pepik Ltd**.

enquiries@pepikbooks.com

www.pepikbooks.com

For Amy, Irie and Max

1. CRASH BANG

It is the middle of the night. I am woken up by an enormous explosion. When I look out of the window I see my dad. He is coughing and choking and he is coming out of the garden shed.

My name is Isabelle Bright and I am eleven. This is the moment I realise that my dad is not like other dads.

My brother, Moz, rushes into the bedroom. 'What on earth was that?' he cries. He joins me at the window. My big sister, Alice, twin sister to Moz, stirs in her top bunk but doesn't bother to get up.

'It's just Dad,' she says, as if it happens every night.

My brother and I try to make out what is going on in the moonlight outside. We can see Dad, calmer now, taking big, deep breaths with his hands on his knees.

'What's that?' I say, pointing to a big black box by Dad's side.

'Dunno,' says Moz, 'but I reckon that's what exploded.'

The box has plumes of thick dark smoke coming out of it. Dad is trying to keep out of the smoke, but he is still standing very close to the box, as if he doesn't want to let it out of his sight.

Moz opens the window and calls out, 'Dad, are you OK?'

'Yes, thanks, Son,' he calls back. 'No problems. Go back to bed.'

Just then, the garden is flooded with light. We see the box more clearly. It is a dark, weighty cube and it has wires pointing out of the top. It doesn't look that exciting, kind of like a big battery, but nevertheless Dad shiftily moves across so that he is standing right in front of it.

A pink vision appears in the garden. It is my mum in a fluffy, pink dressing gown. She has turned on all the lights downstairs. 'Are you OK, Stan?'

'What are you doing, Laverne?' shouts Dad. 'Turn the lights off. Do you want everyone to see?'

'It's late, Stan. Go to bed,' she sighs.

'You too, kids' she calls up at us. We go back to bed.

--

The next morning, when Alice and I go down for breakfast, everything is exactly normal again.

'Dad...' I start, but Mum gives me a look that says, 'Don't you dare mention last night.' So I don't say anything.

Dad beams at us over a big steaming cup of black coffee. 'Good morning, poppets. You sleep OK?'

He looks tired and a bit dirty, but he has a huge grin on his face.

'Yes, thanks,' says Alice. I don't think she remembers last night at all. Right now she is looking tired and dishevelled in her lemon cupcake pyjamas. This is her natural look. But now that she is thirteen, she will go upstairs and spend ages in front of the mirror making herself look perfect. Her long dark hair will be pulled into two tidy plaits and she will have tried on almost everything in her wardrobe before putting on her favourite floaty dress.

I help Mum by laying the table. I get out the cereal and the milk and make everyone a glass of orange juice. Mum is in a rush as she needs to go to work soon. But Moz, Alice and I have all the time in the world. It's the school holidays and the sun is shining.

I have been up for hours. But unlike my sister, I haven't spent my time making myself look fancy. I'm wearing denim shorts and a faded t-shirt, my most comfy clothes. I've tied back my curly blond hair into a ponytail as best I can, but I know it's still messy. Oh well. No, I've been up for hours using the computer, chatting to some of my friends on Facebook. I've got Facebook friends from all over the world. Whatever time of day it is there's always someone about for a chat. I can happily spend all day watching videos or playing games with my mates. Moz and Alice don't understand at all. That's why my Facebook friends are so great. They really get me.

Mum's phone beeps. 'Time to go,' she says.

Dad gives Mum a quick peck on the cheek. 'I'm off too,' he says, gesturing towards his shed. Dad quit his real job a while ago to work on something important in his shed. 'I'm going to be pretty busy today, kids, so please don't disturb me.'

'Bye,' shouts Mum as she heads out of the door. 'Don't get up to any mischief. And please, Belle, try not to spend ALL day indoors.'

2. A VERY STRANGE THINGAMAJIG

Dora and John come round after breakfast. They are our next door neighbours and we see them practically every day, especially in the summer holidays when we are all bored and hot. Dora is thirteen, just like Alice and Moz. Dora and Alice are best friends forever. It can get a bit much sometimes.

But that's OK, because this summer I am mainly hanging out with Moz and John. Moz is my big brother and he's pretty cool. He is enjoying lazing around at home and in the garden, getting a tan. I think this is because he likes to take his t-shirt off all the time to show the girls his cool bod! He has got a lot taller suddenly this year and looks strong and athletic. But I think he's still a bit of a kid inside, wanting to hang out with me and John rather than try and talk to all the cool girls and not knowing what to say. The down-side is that as he's the eldest, he's always bossing us around. He ALWAYS thinks he knows best.

John is eleven, like me. He's OK most of the time, but he can be very annoying too. He always wants me to play his silly games. I'm much more grown up than him and sometimes I just want to go off and chat to my friends on the internet instead.

It's going to be another hot, hot day. After breakfast I'm keen to go onto Facebook. I know my friend Francis from South Africa will be online and

I've got some questions for him. We're designing a new game for the iPhone together. I'm very excited.

But Dad and Moz have started teasing me about how much time I'm spending inside on the computer. And Moz starts up now. "Belle, don't go inside and play on your boring, old computer again. Stay outside in the sunshine." So I say I'll stay, but only for five minutes.

We are amongst the beds in our vegetable garden and suddenly John jumps on top of me. 'You are IT,' he cries.

I sigh. I shrug. And then I run after him. Fast. 'Got you back. Ha ha ha ha.'

I dart off and run on through the beds. Our whole garden is full of vegetable beds. And some of the plants are now very high, so there are loads of places to hide. I run behind the pea plants, but he can still see me through the leaves, so I run off and land next to Alice and Dora in between the thorny raspberries.

'Look, Belle, we've found some raspberries that are already ripe. They're so nice.' Alice picks one for me. I taste its sweet raspberriness.

'Yum. Are there more?'

'Not yet. But soon there'll be loads.'

'Got you,' yells John as he runs down the path. He checks us all out deciding who best to make IT. He gives me a look and I know it's going to be me. So I leap up and run off while he clambers over my sister and Dora. I run quickly, darting between the overgrown potatoes and into the poly-tunnel for the tomatoes.

I take a few deep breaths as I emerge from the other end of the poly-tunnel. Looks like I've finally lost John, so I slow down and look around. Dad's shed is in front of me and I can hear him gently tinkering inside. I'm never sure what he's doing in there, but he's so busy he doesn't notice me or anything that goes on outside the shed. I've given up wondering what he's up to in there. And there's no point trying to ask him. There's no way he'll tell any of us or even let us through the door. 'Top secret. Important work. Right now you're safer not knowing.'

So I ignore Dad and for the first time notice my brother who is trying rather unsuccessfully to climb up one corner of the shed.

'Moz, what are you up to?' I shout.

'Sssh. Quick! Come over here. I need you.'

'What are you doing?'

'Trying to get to that.'

'What?'

'That,' he points up to the top corner of the shed and I see something shiny poking out from the corner of the roof.

'What is it?' I ask.

'No idea. But it looks weird don't you think?'

'Yes. Is it a kind of ball?'

'Not sure. And how did it get there? I want to have a closer look. Help me. Here.'

He crouches down with his arms stretching out horizontally, resting on the shed. 'Climb onto my shoulders and I'll try and lift you up.' I climb onto his back and lever myself as carefully as I can so that I'm sitting on his shoulders. He slowly stands up.

'You're heavy,' he moans.

'Shut up. This was YOUR idea. I can't reach anyway. I'm still too low.'

'Can you stand up on my shoulders? I'll hold your legs.'

I feel rather unsteady, but I try one foot at a time. Just as I'm trying to get my second leg to balance on his shoulder, I reach up and can just grab onto the side of the roof and I get my balance.

'I'm there.'

'Excellent, Belle. Can you see it?'

'Yep. It's shiny, but it's only half a ball and it's kind of bleeping.'

'Really? That's odd. Can you reach it and pull it down?'

I reach up and grab it. It's cold in my hands. And although it looks like I could easily lift it off – it's only the size of a tennis ball after all – I can't seem to lift it. It's like it's glued down or something. As I try and pull it, I start to wobble and kind of collapse onto Moz's head.

'It's no use. I can't lift it,' I wail at Moz as we both tumble down to the ground.

'I really want to see it,' he says. 'Can you lift me?'

14

I look at him. He's about ten centimetres taller than me and tonnes heavier. 'Absolutely no way.'

'Fair enough,' he grins. 'New plan. You can take a picture with your iPhone.'

So I climb back onto Moz's shoulders again and manage, just, to take a photo without wobbling too much.

Lying on the grass, we both examine the picture in more detail.

'What is it?' asks Moz.

'Well, it's definitely electronic, but other than that, I've no idea. Do you think Dad knows it's there?'

'I don't think so. What do we do now?'

Then I have a brainwave, 'I know. I know. We'll ask my friends on Facebook. One of them is bound to know.'

I quickly email the photo to my Facebook account along with a status message saying: 'Anyone know what this is? We've just found it on top of our shed. It's metal and cold and seems to be bleeping.'

'Now what?' asks Moz.

'We wait, I guess,' I reply and we start to walk indoors.

3. FRAN THE SPIDER

We don't have to wait for very long. We have barely got inside the door when I my phone blips to say I've got a Facebook message. It's from my friend Francis in South Africa. Sometimes I do worry about him, he must ALWAYS be online. But he's there when we need him today.

We go straight to the computer. It's faster than the iPhone and has got two screens so Moz and I can both look at it together. I go onto Facebook and click on Fran's name in Chat. Fran's nick is 'Fran the Spider'. I asked him once why he's got a nickname rather than his real name and he said he didn't like people knowing too much about him. But why 'Fran the Spider' I asked? He just laughed and said he wasn't telling. One day I'll get it out of him.

> **Fran the Spider>** Yo Belle. How ya doing? What have you been up to?
> **Belle>** Hey Francis. Glad you're there. Yeah its strange isn't it? Moz and I just found it on top of Dad's shed.
> **Fran the Spider>** I've got an idea what it is but you're not going to like it. I think its one of these...http://www.sdotldotu. com/mini-satellite-105

I go straight to the link he has sent me and there is indeed a picture of the thing on top of the shed. It looks like it's in some kind of catalogue: there's a photo, description and price.

The mini satellite 105 is our best-selling satellite dish. Only 5cm in diameter it can broadcast a good quality TV signal direct to your computer. Being so small it is virtually invisible and a must for all kinds of spying. Best of all, at a new low price of £29.99, it's within every spy's budget.

'Spying!' say Moz and I together.

'Who's spying on Dad?' I ask, 'and why would they want to?'

'He's very secretive about his work,' says Moz, 'maybe it's really important.'

'But it's just Dad.' It doesn't really make much sense to me at all. Dad has been tinkering in the shed for as long as we can remember. Is his work really so important that someone would want to spy on him? And what on earth do we do now?

Fran the Spider> Hello? You still there?
Belle> Yep. We're just trying to work it out. Why is there a satellite dish on our shed? And is someone really spying on us?
Fran the Spider> Its really freaky. You sure its the thing you found?
Belle> Definitely.
Fran the Spider> I've been looking at the website that it's on.
Belle> And?
Fran the Spider> I can't make much sense of it. You need a password to access most of it. The only thing that isn't password protected is the catalogue of gadgets. And they're all for spying and surveillance. Really cool stuff actually.
Belle> This is serious, Fran. How do we find out more? And what sort of name is SDOTLDOTU? Its pretty rubbish.
Fran the Spider> I can't work it out either. I'll keep looking for you and let you know if I find something.

Moz has been browsing the website on the other screen while I've been chatting to Fran. Suddenly he stops and points at the screen.

'Look at this Belle,' he almost shouts in excitement. 'Look at the bottom of the page in tiny, tiny letters.'

I look at where he is pointing:

All items can be viewed and tested at The Gadget Shop.

Just ask for Alec.

'But I know that shop,' I say. 'it's in town.'

'What a coincidence!' says Moz. It will be much, much later when we realise that it isn't a coincidence at all.

4. ON THE ROAD

Moz and I know that the next thing we need to do is go to The Gadget Shop. But we are both very reluctant. I am scared and worried about what we might find. Moz would never admit to being frightened of anything. But I think underneath that's what's stopping him too.

We look out of the kitchen window. Dad has not emerged from the shed all day. We know better than to disturb him when he's working. He's liable to bite anyone's head off who goes near him.

On the other side of the garden Alice and Dora are swinging idly back and forth. They are both immaculately dressed in pretty summer dresses. Their long straight hair is tied in two perfect plaits. The only differences between them are the things they can't change. Alice has dark brown hair and is almost ghostly pale. Dora has perfect blond hair and looks brown and tanned. They are chatting away endlessly. I don't know what they find to discuss all day. They always clam up when I appear. Well, we are about to make their day a whole lot more interesting, whether they like it or not. Because Moz and I have decided that this is too big to keep to ourselves.

--

Alice, Dora, Moz, John and I are all sitting on the grass trying to make a plan. Moz and I have shown them the satellite on the roof and the mysterious SDOTLDOTU website. We all agree that this is a serious situation, but we can't make up our minds what to do next.

'We must go straight to Dad,' says Alice, always the sensible one.

'But he doesn't like to be disturbed,' I say.

'I'm not going in there,' says Moz, pointing at the shed.

'Me neither,' I agree.

'Well…' says Alice. She is obviously thinking about exactly how cross Dad will be if we disturb him.

John has been lying quietly on the ground chewing on a piece of grass. He's obviously been thinking hard and suddenly he stands up and starts to tell us his plan.

'There's only one thing that we can do,' he says with authority, although it's hard to take him seriously as he has a red criss-cross mark on his cheek where he's been lying on the grass. 'We must go to The Gadget Shop straight away. No more messing around. Let's get our bikes now.'

--

There's no argument from any of us and we are quickly on our way. As soon as we turn off our little cul-de-sac we go straight onto the main road into town. The road is completely empty of cars and instead everyone is using bikes. Mum says that you have to be super, super rich to drive a car these days. Petrol is unbelievably expensive, there doesn't seem to be any oil left anywhere in the world and you absolutely need to have oil to make petrol. I love to be able to cycle. Mum would never have trusted me on the roads when there were lots of cars around, but now I'm free to go wherever I want.

The five of us cycle together in a group. Moz is at the front as he likes to lead the way, with me and John quite close behind him. Dora and Alice are dawdling along behind us chatting. One time they get too far behind so Moz cycles right round in a big circle and ends up behind them. Then he rides up behind them quite fast and shouts, 'Hurry along ladies'. Alice pulls a face but they both speed up a little. Satisfied, Moz cycles through them until he is at the front of our little group again.

There is still a cycle lane down the side of the road, but everyone ignores that and cycles down the middle, although we still follow the system of always cycling on the left, so everyone proceeds in quite an orderly fashion. There are loads of cyclists out and about today. There are people going to work, with cycle clips round the legs of their suits. There are families with kids on the back or being pulled along in a trailer. And also there are plenty of grannies and granddads on rickety old bikes with a basket full of shopping in the front.

We are just overtaking a very slow old lady on a bike that looks like it's older than she is when the traffic lights change suddenly and we all screech on our brakes. We have stopped at a pedestrian crossing as a man is crossing the road. He is strangely dressed for such a hot day in a big navy raincoat with the hood up. He is very fat and very sweaty. As the green man flashes and he is almost on the other side he suddenly looks up and cries out in alarm. The old lady on her ancient bike is heading straight for him.

'I've got no brakes,' she shouts as she hits him and knocks him to the ground. We jump off our bikes and hurry over to help.

'You OK?' says Moz to the man who is sprawled rather uncomfortably on the tarmac.

'Fine thanks,' he mumbles as he scrambles to pick up the thing that has fallen out from inside his coat. The thing that has fallen out is actually a laptop, quite a big old-fashioned one that he must have been carrying somehow under his coat. Now that the laptop is on the floor, it is obvious that he isn't fat at all; he was just pretending. But why?

John nudges me and whispers, 'look at his arms.' I look at his arms as he picks up the computer and holds it close to his chest. They look normal, even if what he is doing is not. 'Not those arms!' John says, 'look on the outside of his coat.' And sure enough poking through the cuffs of his coat is another pair of hands. The hands are not moving and I suddenly realise that they are fake, probably prosthetic as they look so realistic.

He looks at us and at the old lady on her bike and decides we're not worth worrying about. He pulls his coat back round him and I notice the silliest badge I have seen in a long time, it says 'I love

SLUgs' with a picture of a big fat slug underneath. Then with his fake arms dangling down, he wanders off. He looks just as he did before, a big fat man in a silly coat.

We check on the old lady and she is not at all bothered by what's happened. I think that (a) she didn't notice the fake arms and (b) she must have run over people before.

'No harm done, dears. Toodle-oo,' she says to us all before wobbling off down the road again.

We have a think about the strange man. Is there anything we should do?

'Call the police?' suggests Alice.

'And say what?' replies Moz. 'We've just seen a man with fake arms? They won't believe us. And I don't think having fake arms is a crime anyway.'

We agree that there is nothing more that we can do and continue cycling into town. We lock up our bikes and go straight to The Gadget Shop.

5. THE GADGET SHOP

The front of the shop is an endless window of flat screen TVs. Each one tuned to the same channel, right now showing the racing. Identical horses gallop across the screens.

The shop has all the latest stuff. Most of which I either have: high-spec computer, iPhone or really want: new Nintendo handheld device. I am gently stroking this and wondering how many weeks of pocket money I'll need to save before I can buy it, when I realise that the others have all gone straight to the counter.

'I'm looking for Alec,' John asks the greasy teenager at the desk.

'Um,' says the young sales assistant gormlessly.

'It is me that you require,' says a short man in a rather shiny suit. He is wearing a badge which says:

'I'm here to help, my name is… ALEC'. (Strangely I notice that at the bottom in brackets and small letters, the mysterious word "SLUrp" has been added in pen.) He doesn't look like he really wants to help anyone, but more like he is forced to do it. 'Can I be of assistance?' he asks smarmily.

'We've found this thing,' says John. 'Show him the picture, Belle.'

I'm not sure whether I want to trust this man, but now I don't feel like I've got any choice, so I show him the photo of the satellite on my iPhone.

Alec's mood changes immediately. A spark lights up in his eyes. I trust him even less.

'Where did you find this?' he demands.

'On top of our shed,' I answer shyly.

'And where, pray, do you live?' he asks.

'Over there,' says John waving his hand and being deliberately vague.

Luckily, it seems like Alec has given up on this line of questioning and concentrates on the picture on my iPhone.

'Come into my office,' he says.

Office is perhaps a bit of a grand term for an oversized, dusty old cupboard. We all manage to squeeze in, just, and he firmly shuts the door. The room has got shelves floor to ceiling, each crammed full of technical gadgets. Some of them look rather familiar.

'Now the mini-satellite 105,' he says. 'Yes, I've sold a number of those.'

'We'd like to know who bought it from you?' says John.

'Would you now? Well, that'll cost you,' he says meanly.

Glumness sets in. We don't have any money.

Seeing our faces he says nastily, 'I'm sure we can come to some arrangement.' A shiver goes down my spine. I don't like this man at all.

While he is talking he is looking up the satellite on a website.

'That's the SDOTLDOTU website,' says John.

Alec grins. 'Well yes, it is. But that's not how you say it.'

'How do you say it?' asks John.

'Ah, that would be telling. It's a kind of code. But it IS my website. I sell all these gadgets online.' He gestures round the room to all the items stacked up on the shelves, 'as well as directly in the shop, obviously.'

'So can you tell us who bought OUR satellite?' asks John.

'Most probably. But what's in it for me?' Alec sneers.

We look at each other. We don't have anything to offer him.

'Come on. You must have something. Could you bring me the satellite from your shed?'

That would be easy.

Moz says, 'Yes of course. The satellite. We'll bring it in tomorrow.'

'No problem,' says Alec and he opens the door and gestures for us to leave.

'No. No,' says Moz. 'We need the information now.'

'Well, that would be stupid of me, wouldn't it? As if you'd ever bring me the satellite then.'

'We would. We would,' we all chime.

'No chance,' he says, 'unless…' I realise he is looking at me, more specifically he is looking at the iPhone in my hands.

'Oh no,' I say, 'not my iPhone.'

29

'You can have it back as soon as you return the satellite,' he says.

I shake my head but everyone else is looking at me. 'You'd get it back,' says John. 'Go on, it's the only way.'

Very, very reluctantly I hand the phone over to Alec.

'Thank you, child,' he says, making me even madder. 'And now for the information you seek.'

He turns back to his computer and the SDOTL-DOTU website. After a few clicks of his mouse he reveals some hidden information about everyone who has bought the Mini-satellite 105.

'Very interesting,' he says, 'very, very interesting. It looks like someone came in and bought ten of these a week ago. Nothing since.'

'It must be them then,' says John.

'And it must be someone local,' says Alice, 'as they came into the shop.'

Alice hasn't said a word since we came in.

'Clever girl,' says Alec. 'Do you want to know who it was?'

He keeps us hanging on for a few more seconds as he checks the website.

'It was someone from Conch Oil,' he says finally. 'You know, the big oil company.'

'Huh?' we say as it makes no sense.

'Didn't your dad use to work for them?' John asks me.

'Yes. But that doesn't explain why they would put a satellite on his roof, does it?'

'No,' says John, thinking out loud. 'Surely their job is to look for oil, not to spy on people. Why are they interested in YOUR dad?'

'But what does an oil company do if they can't find any oil? Wouldn't they just go bust?' asks Alice.

'Another good question, young lady,' answers Alec. Alice squirms uncomfortably.

'Conch Oil seems to be getting up to all sorts of things these days. No one seems to be sure,' he says. 'I've been getting all sorts of strange reports.'

'That doesn't explain why they're interested in Dad though,' says Moz.

'Indeed,' says Alec. 'Maybe he's doing something they're interested in? They're getting pretty desperate to find something that could replace petrol.'

I think of Dad working away in his shed. Could he really be working on something so important? Luckily, we are all smart enough not to say anything to Alec. And we all look at him with our best blank faces.

'Thank you. I think we'll be going now,' says Moz in his most grown-up voice.

'Any time,' says Alec, 'don't forget the satellite will you?' He waves the iPhone at me and smirks.

We all file out of the door and he swings it shut behind us immediately. We walk as calmly as we can out of the shop, but as soon as we get out of the door we all begin to run fast. We don't stop until we get back to our bikes.

'Phew!' says Moz as we all gasp for breath.

6. A SHADOWY FIGURE

It's getting late when we get back home. We are all starving and I hope Mum will be home, so we can have some tea. I wonder if Mum or Dad has missed us at all. As I cycle up our road I realise that Mum's bike isn't back, so she must still be at work. Dad is probably in the shed – he never normally comes out until Mum absolutely insists.

Dora and John go back to their house and Alice, Moz and I park our bikes on the front lawn and head in our front door. The house is empty and I feel a bit sad that after such an exciting day, no one is here to greet us.

It's only when we've eaten several biscuits each that we notice for the first time that it is not as quiet in the garden as it is in the house. We hear voices coming from somewhere near the back of the garden. Maybe Mum is home after all? It doesn't sound like Mum though. It sounds like two men arguing. The door to Dad's shed is almost hidden at this time of year behind all our vegetables. We go out into the garden straight away and head towards the pea plants as they are the tallest. We are now close enough to almost hear what they are saying. As we had guessed one of the men is Dad. He is standing in front of the shed with his back pressed against the door. He definitely doesn't want the other man to even glimpse inside. The other man is short and rather fat and is wearing a crumpled old raincoat with some red converse boots.

We can't quite hear what they are saying until Dad suddenly raises his voice and says, 'Look Bob. The truth is I just don't believe you. Leave me alone.' And with that Dad opens the door of the shed as little as possible and slides inside. He closes and locks the door behind him. The second man, Bob, looks like he is wondering what to do next. He looks back towards the shed one more time and I am sure that he is looking straight at the satellite dish. Finally he shrugs, turns back towards the house and starts to walk out of the garden. As he passes the vegetable garden, we manage to sneak round to the other side of the peas so he doesn't notice we are there. He walks down the side of our house, opens our side gate and disappears down the street.

'What do you make of that?' asks Moz.

'I've never seen anyone visit Dad in his shed before. Doesn't look like Dad liked it much either, does it?' replies Alice.

'Did anyone else see him looking at the satellite?' I ask, 'I'm sure he was looking straight at it.'

'Yes,' says Alice, 'I think he put it there too.'

'Do you think he was from Conch Oil?' I ask.

'I don't know,' says Moz. 'He didn't look like he was from Conch Oil. And I thought he wasn't very happy when he noticed the satellite.'

'He knew exactly what it was though,' I say.

'Yes. Definitely,' agree the twins.

--

Mum shouts at us from the kitchen, 'Does anyone want any tea?'

She's home from work at last. We jump up from behind the peas, 'Yessssssss,' we yell.

Half an hour later our whole family is sitting at the table. Mum has made fish, chips and peas. It is lovely to be back to normal and I scoff everything on my plate in record-quick time.

'You're all a bit quiet this evening,' comments Mum.

It's true that none of us can be bothered to say much. We're all worn out and Moz, Alice and I have agreed that we shouldn't mention what has happened today. Mum will only worry.

'Just tired, Mum,' says Moz.

She seems happy with that and starts to make us some pudding. 'This will cheer you up,' she says as she puts fresh strawberries and blueberries in our bowls from the garden and adds a huge scoop of ice cream to each one.

Dad isn't that chatty either. When Mum asks him what he's been up to all day he just grunts and gestures towards the shed. He doesn't mention his visitor and I'm pretty sure he doesn't want Mum to know. As well as looking very tired and pale, he also looks fidgety and on edge. He keeps drumming his fingers on the table in a really fast, annoying way.

'Right then you guys,' announces Mum. 'I'm going upstairs for a bath. Can you all clear up for me?'

We all protest but she puts her foot down straight away. 'I've had an exhausting day at work. Not like you guys mucking about.' When she says this she looks first at me, Moz and Alice and then at Dad, as if he's been mucking about too.

We all stop protesting and she wanders upstairs for a bath, whistling a happy tune to herself.

--

Alice and I clear the plates and stack the dishwasher while Dad washes and Moz dries the pans. We are aching with curiosity about Dad's strange visitor and Moz can't stop himself from asking Dad about him.

'Dad…' says Moz.

'Yes, son.'

'Is your work really important?'

Dad looks at Moz in surprise. None of us have ever taken an interest in Dad's work before.

'It is. Yes, it definitely is. I'm just at a really exciting time as well.'

'Is that why you don't want anyone to see what you're doing?' queries Moz innocently.

Dad squints at Moz as he wonders what he's getting at.

'I have to keep it a secret. Otherwise other people might try and steal it.'

'Like that man who was here today? Bob?' blurts out Moz.

Dad eyes open wide, 'You saw him?'

'Yes,' we all say. Dad turns to find that Alice and I have both stopped what we are doing and are staring at him intently.

Alice leads the way. 'Dad, there's something we've got to tell you. Come and sit down.'

We all gather round the table and start to fill Dad in on our day. We draw a picture of the satellite, as the photo is still on my iPhone. We point to the satellite on his shed; we can even see it glimmering slightly in the setting sun. Finally we tell him all about our visit to The Gadget Shop and what Alec told us about Conch Oil. Dad is completely silent while we talk. He only speaks up once when I mention Alec taking my iPhone, 'That little creep,' he says.

When we've told him everything, Dad stays silent for a little longer and looks from Alice's face, to Moz's, and lastly to mine. He is thinking hard about what to do. 'Maybe we can help, Dad,' says Alice gently.

At last he gets up, goes over to the kitchen door and shuts it firmly.

'You can't tell anyone about this, not even Mum,' he says.

We agree quickly.

'I've invented something,' he says, speaking quietly and confidently. 'something that may well change the world. But it looks like someone else wants my idea. And thanks to you guys, I now know who it is – Conch. Bob tried to warn me.'

'But,' I say, boiling over with excitement. 'What is it, Dad? What have you invented?'

'You'll see,' says Dad. When he sees our disappointed faces though, he adds, 'Tonight. You'll see tonight.'

Just then we hear Mum's footsteps as she starts to come downstairs. Quick as a flash we all jump up and take up our positions clearing up the kitchen.

'Have you lot not finished yet?' she cries as she comes into the kitchen.

'Nearly done, Mum,' says Alice.

'I'm going to watch TV,' says Mum. 'Please leave my kitchen spick and span.'

'Of course,' reassures Moz, 'you go and put your feet up.'

Mum looks a little suspicious; Moz isn't normally so thoughtful. But she does as she's told.

As soon as we can hear the TV and with the kitchen cleaned up just enough to stop Mum from shouting at us, Moz quickly shuts the kitchen door and we again gather round the kitchen table.

Now Dad has a plan.

'We need to test my invention,' he explains. 'I thought it could wait, but now I know it has to be tonight. We need some open space to do the test. I know the perfect place, but it's right on the very edge of town, about 10 miles away.'

'How will we get there?' asks Moz.

'Bikes, of course. Leave it to me. I'll get it set up as soon as Mum is asleep, then I'll call for you.'

'What about Dora and John?' asks Alice.

'Yes of course. We'll need them too. Can you phone John?' he asks me.

'Not without my iPhone,' I say.

'I'll do it,' says Alice, picking up her mobile and quickly dialling Dora.

After Alice has filled Dora and John in on the plan, we all troop into the sitting room and watch TV with Mum. After a few minutes we all start to yawn and stretch.

'I'm really tired,' says Alice, 'I'm going to bed.'

'Me too,' I say and Moz follows us up as well.

Dad catches us on the stairs, 'Get some rest,' he says, 'I'll wake you up when it's safe.'

I have a wash and clean my teeth and then jump into bed in everything except my shoes. I think there's no chance that I'll sleep I'm far too excited and nervous about tonight. But moments after getting into bed, I must have dropped off because the next thing I realise, Dad is gently shaking me and whispering, 'Wake up, darling, it's time to go.'

Bleary-eyed but ready, Alice and I join Dad in Moz's room. 'Come and look,' says Dad, pulling back the curtains.

We peer out of the window. It is a dark night and the moon is nowhere to be seen. A street-light down the road provides the only light – a pale orange glow. As our eyes grow accustomed to the darkness, we can make out something on our drive.

It's large. It has wheels. Hang on a second. It's our car.

7. SLED TEAM

We take a lantern and go out and examine the car with Dad. I haven't seen our car for a while, now that I think about it. We haven't used it for ages because of the petrol problem and now I realise Dad has been hiding it in his shed.

'What are we going to do with it now Dad?' asks Moz.

'We are going to test it,' says Dad.

'What. You mean it actually works. Without petrol?'

'Yep. Hope so anyway.' says Dad, both proudly and nervously at the same time. 'But first we need to get it to a big open space where we can test it in peace.'

We look at the car. It's heavy. Surely he isn't expecting us to push it?

'Don't worry,' says Dad. 'I've got a plan. Look.' He takes us round to the front of the car and there are five ropes tied there. Attached to the other end of each rope is a bike. Our bikes. One for each of us.

'Hop on,' says Dad gleefully. 'I've got it all worked out, so you should be perfectly balanced. You'll be like a team of dogs pulling a sledge. A sled team.'

I'm not sure if I like the idea of being in a team of dogs. Everyone else look a bit unsure, too. But we do as we're told. For now.

Moz's bike is in the middle as he's the strongest; followed by Alice and Dora one on each side and finally John and I are positioned on the outside.

'I'll ride in the car, of course,' says Dad, 'so that I can steer. Now go forward on your bikes until the ropes are taut. That's it. Now I'll get in, and you should start pedalling on the beep of the horn.'

I catch Moz's eye. Is this really going to work? He shrugs. Dad is definitely crazy. But is he crazy mad or crazy clever?

Dad honks the horn, and we start to pedal. At first it seems like the car isn't going to move at all, but with a strong tug it jolts into action. The car starts moving, slowly and juddery at first. Dad shouts out of the window, 'Don't think about the car, I'm steering that. Just keep pedalling in a straight line, and don't let your rope get loose.'

We head off down our road. It's not that hard to cycle and pull at the same time. Suddenly, Moz, who is at the front, shouts 'Stop!' and we all slam on our brakes. The car keeps going for another metre or two and I think it is going to hit Moz, until Dad manages to pull hard on the handbrake and the car screeches to a halt too.

'What's up, Son?' says Dad sounding a bit exasperated and Moz replies, sounding a bit exasperated too. 'You haven't told us where we are going.'

It turns out we are going to the airport. Or at least what used to be the airport. Now it's just a big empty field of tarmac. Perfect for testing the car.

It's quite a way off though, over ten miles. It's easy,' says Dad. 'Moz, you know the way to the motorway, don't you?' Moz nods. 'Get on the motorway and just follow the signs to the airport.'

'Won't there be any cars?' I ask.

'I doubt it,' replies Dad. 'We'll just cycle over to the side and hide in the verge if we see or hear one.'

With our bike lights all on full beam, we set off through our deserted neighbourhood. It is very, very quiet. It feels eerie cycling along like this, like many eyes are watching me.

I concentrate on the road again. It's lucky that we are unlikely to see any other vehicles on our journey as we are taking up the whole of the road with our triangle of cyclists followed by our large unlikely package.

Soon enough we are going round a huge roundabout (bit tricky steering the car, but we manage) and heading down the slip road onto the motorway. It's a long, long time since I've been on a motorway, but it just looks exactly the same, just without any cars on it. The signs are still blue with white writing, and we see one that says "Airport 5 miles", so we know we are on the right track.

--

It is lovely, cycling down the motorway. The road is flat and straight and we are all pedalling fast. As we are pulling the car between the five of us, it doesn't take much more effort than just cycling normally and we are zipping down the road with the warm wind blowing in our faces.

Moz shouts back to Dad, 'Why can't we just test the car here Dad? There's plenty of room.'

Dad looks around as if he is seriously considering it. The road is totally empty and we haven't seen anything for miles and miles.

'No,' says Dad, 'there still might be a car, you know. It's not completely impossible.'

He is proved right just a few minutes later when I hear a faint rumbling behind us. It doesn't sound like a car though. As we carry on it gets louder and louder. I turn around and I can definitely see two bright white lights glowing in the distance behind us. Headlights.

'Pull over. Pull over,' I yell and we all start to steer into the verge. There is a slight dip beside the road and Dad shouts, 'Lights off. Then untie the bikes and pull them down into the ditch.'

Everyone else unties the rope from their bikes no problem, but my knot is so tight that I can't undo it.

'Quickly,' shouts Dad as we can clearly see something approaching now and it looks like there are more than one.

'I can't do it.'

Moz comes to help, but the knot is too tight. In the end we just push the bike under the car with all the ropes and hope they don't notice it.

'What about the car?' John asks Dad.

'Well it can't go down the ditch.' says Dad, "It's too steep. We'll just have to leave it on the side of the road and hopefully they'll just think it's been deserted when it ran out of petrol.'

With that he takes my hand and we all jump down into the ditch.

Seconds later the motorway is buzzing with a huge number of vehicles. Leading the way are three police cars. There are no sirens but all their lights are blazing. Behind them and surrounded by five more security guards on motorbikes is a huge tanker of oil. As it passes our hiding place we see that on the side of the tanker is a picture of a spiral conch seashell and in massive letters the words CONCH OIL.

'Well I never,' mutters Dad. 'That tanker must be full of oil.'

The vehicles pass our car without slowing down or even seeming to notice it and we breathe a huge sigh of relief. When they finally pass out of view and the road is silent once more, we drag the bikes out of the ditch and rig up our formation for cycling in the same way as before.

--

The road is deathly quiet again for a couple more miles. We are less comfortable this time and more nervous. I keep looking over my shoulder, just in case another vehicle is approaching, but there's nothing. Soon we see a sign that reads, "Services 1 mile".

'That must have closed down by now,' says Moz. 'There's no one to use it.'

But as we reach the road that goes off to the service station, we realise he is wrong. At the entrance to the services is a huge electronic sign and it says in huge red glowing letters, "Petrol available here. Only £99.99 per litre." The £99.99 is flashing garishly.

We all slow down and finally stop just by the sign.

Dad gets out of the car. 'Wow,' he says, 'Does it really cost that much now? No wonder no one can afford it.'

'Is it really that much?' I ask.

It's one hundred times more than it used to be.' says Dad.

I look away from the road and up the hill to the service station. It has its lights on and I can faintly hear people talking on the breeze.

Alice hears it too. 'Everyone, sssh,' she says, 'I think there are people up there.'

We leave the bikes and car in darkness and cross over the carriageway to get a better look. We can't see exactly what's going on but we can see enough. There is the tanker and all the accompanying security.

'They're refuelling the petrol station,' says Moz, 'I bet that doesn't happen very often.'

'No,' says Dad.

'Let's get out of here,' says Dora and we all agree. We jump on our bikes and we are off.

But our mood has changed. We pedal quickly and silently until we reach the airport.

8. FASTER, DAD, FASTER

We know that we've arrived at the airport when the road suddenly stops. In front of us is a hastily built, barbed wire fence. We turn off our bike lights and our eyes grow a bit more accustomed to the night. It is not completely dark. The sky is a navy blue rather than pitch black. The moon is trying to peek out from behind some clouds and gives a ghostly grey glow to everything in front of us. There is a huge building just behind the fence, towering and black with no lights on anywhere.

'I think,' says Dad, 'that that is the terminal, where all the passengers go before boarding their plane.'

'It hasn't been used in a while,' comments Alice.

'No, flying is even more expensive than driving now. It uses even more petrol.'

John is using his bike light to explore the fence, looking for a way through.

'Here we go,' he calls after only a minute.

Sure enough when we all go over to look, the fence has been pulled apart. It looks like it's been used as a shortcut.

'Not very secure,' Moz says.

'I don't think anyone cares,' says Dad and we all push our bikes through. The car is slightly more difficult. We tug on the fence from both sides to make the gap bigger. Then, when Dad starts to get in the car saying, 'I'll steer,' Moz stops him and says 'No, we'll need you to push. Let Belle steer.'

Dad agrees. 'Get comfy, Belle,' he instructs. 'Seat belt on and when you're ready take the hand-brake off.'

Dad, Moz and John are behind the car huffing and puffing as they push. Alice and Dora are on either side of the car, holding the front wing mirrors and pushing a bit while also trying to give me instructions.

'Left a bit. No right. Stop. Too far.'

Eventually we get the car lined up with the gap in the fence. The boys heave with all their might and we roll through the gap. After we're through the fence, it's tough-going as we are trying to roll the car over rough grass. Then suddenly it's easy. We've hit the tarmac and the car rolls off almost effortlessly. It takes everyone by surprise and Dad, Moz and John fall flat on their faces as the car and I drift slowly off into the centre of the runway. I put on the handbrake and get out of the car.

'We're here.' I say as I help Dad and the boys to their feet.

--

Moz shines his bike light down the tarmac. We are right at the bottom end of a long, long runway that stretches off into the distance. On one side of the runway there is the terminal building and on the other side we can see the flight control tower. It is a distinctive shape: thin at the bottom with a big wide top. Round the top there is a ring of dark windows, some of them glinting in the moonlight. But there is no sign of life, it looks dark and deserted.

'This is perfect,' says Dad. 'I'm going to get started.' He is already rummaging round in the boot of the car, which is stuffed with equipment and tools. It looks like we've been dragging half the contents of his shed down the motorway.

'What do you want us to do, Dad?' asks Moz.

'Get yourself comfy, I think, while I set up… the show is about to begin!'

We don't need to be told that twice. We find some old boxes and crates amongst the litter that is strewn on the grass and arrange them at the side of the runway. Moz, John and I lounge on the crates. It's been a long night and it's not over yet. Then my sister and Dora start to pull a feast of snacks from their backpacks. There are crisps, biscuits, chocolate and cans of drink. I discover I'm ravenously hungry; it's been a long time since tea.

After I've eaten, I take some food over to Dad. He waves it away. He is completely focussed on what he is doing and there's no stopping him now. We don't mind. We are here and we are ready to finally see what he has to show us.

--

Dad spends a long time getting the car ready. From the boot he has pulled lots of different tools.

Most are familiar like screwdrivers, wrenches and a blow torch. There are also plenty of laptops, wires and electronic-type devices. When he has everything lined up next to the car he opens up the bonnet and turns on a huge lantern. Then he starts tinkering. He wires up one of the laptops so it is attached to the engine under the bonnet and starts to scribble down lots of information in a scruffy little notebook he has pulled from his pocket. He adjusts a few settings on the computer and again starts scribbling frantically.

At last he is ready and he gestures for us to gather round.

'This,' he announces as we all huddle round the open bonnet and stare in at a familiar but rather ordinary looking black box, 'is our engine.'

'Is that what exploded in our shed?' I ask innocently.

'Well, yes.' He hesitates and then continues very quickly, 'But I've fixed that problem now and we should really just get on, shouldn't we?'

He starts again in an altogether more commanding voice. 'This is no ordinary engine that runs on petrol. This is a completely new type of engine that's never been used in a car before.'

He waits. We wait silently.

'This is the world's first NUCLEAR CAR.'

We all gasp.

'Dad, that's ridiculous,' says Moz. 'Nuclear energy comes from huge power stations, you can't do it at home. It would be far, far too dangerous.'

'True. Nuclear energy can be dangerous. But that's why I've spent all this time getting it right. If it was easy, everyone would have done it, wouldn't they?'

Moz shuts up.

'It's all very complicated,' he begins. 'The trick is to make the energy slowly in a controlled way. The other important thing is to stop the nuclear fuel escaping. The fuel is a special type of rock that lasts for hundreds of years. The rock is then wrapped in an amazing new type of plastic made of quartz and diamonds to make sure every single tiny bit of the nuclear fuel stays safely inside.'

This all sounds kind of sensible, I guess. But then he says, 'Now the only really dangerous bit is starting the engine.'

'Starting the engine?' says Alice in alarm. 'But isn't that what you need to do now?'

'Don't worry, chicken,' he says, 'I am well prepared.'

And with that he opens the door to the back seat of the car and pulls out a heavy lead vest (like the kind a nurse might use when doing an x-ray) and a massive helmet with a glass visor as thick as double glazing.

'Now go and stand behind those crates while I start this baby up. You'll have to duck down while I start the engine, but after that you can watch.'

We retreat to our watching place behind the crates and Dad puts on his protective clothing and huge helmet. From the pile beside the car he picks up his blowtorch (so that's what it's for) and lights it with a match. The blow torch burns first with a bright orange glow, and then concentrates to a hotter fluorescent blue colour. Dad looks at the car and the open bonnet. Then he turns to us and shouts, 'Get ready.' We duck down.

We can hear a few clunks and clicks, but nothing like an engine starting. We keep waiting. And then suddenly there is a high-pitched roar accompanied by a bright yellow light. The light fills the whole sky for several seconds, turning night temporarily into day. Then it dies away to darkness again. We peek out from behind the crates. Dad is throwing off his visor and jacket and jumping into the open door of the car. With a rather disappointing dull whizz instead of the expected roar, he is off, heading down the runway.

We follow him onto the runway. He's not going that fast yet and we start to run after him. Moz and John cheer. 'Go Dad,' shouts Alice. The car is picking up speed and zooming off into the distance. We can no longer keep up and stop, breathing quickly. Dad turns on the headlights and the runway is illuminated in front of him. He's getting faster and faster.

'Maybe he's going to take off,' jokes John.

He reaches the end of the runway and does a handbrake turn, screeching on the brakes and releasing them as soon as he is pointed back down the tarmac again. This time he is pointing right at us and the headlights get brighter and brighter. He is approaching very fast and suddenly he is coming straight at us. We watch in horror, unable

54

to move, he is coming towards us at an incredible speed. Only just in time he swerves off round us. We are safe but now he has lost control and is heading right into the crates at the side of the runway. Again we hear the squeal of brakes and then the tumbling of boxes as Dad crashes through the crates and into the grass and rubbish.

He has stopped and now he emerges triumphant. 'Did you see that? That was awesome. It works! It works!'

We run over to him. Moz slaps him on the back in a big manly way and I simply give him a big huge hug. Alice and Dora are jumping around in excitement.

'Oh, Dad. That's so amazing! I can't believe it,' shouts Alice.

Dad pats his car. 'Well done, car.'

Moz finds one of our cans of drink from the side of the runway and shakes it enthusiastically before spraying it all over both the car and ourselves.

'Not on the car,' Dad laughs, 'this car is going to change the world. You'll see.'

We're all lost in the moment, giggling and shouting and dancing around. We can only see as far as each other and the car in the light of the lantern.

Then our world changes in an instant. We are suddenly surrounded by five bright lights and the roar of engines. There are motorbikes approaching from all sides.

9. THE MEN IN BLACK

Within seconds they are upon us. The sound of the motorbike engines is deafening, the headlights blinding. We huddle together around the car, and I look to Dad for support. He looks pale and worried too, but he whispers, 'Don't worry. They won't hurt us. They just want to scare us.'

I feel a little bit better, but there is no denying that I am very afraid. I grab Moz's hand and he holds it tight. And then we wait.

When the men can get no closer, they form a ring of bikes around us. They shut off their engines and suddenly there is silence. No one says anything. One by one they turn off their headlights except the one directly in front of us. He leaves his light on, shining straight at Dad. They dismount their bikes and stand beside them. Each is clad from head to toe in black leather. On their heads they are wearing black helmets and their visors are down. There is no sign of the human beings underneath at all.

The biggest man, who is standing directly in front of us, raises his visor just enough for us to hear him speak. His mouth is narrow and wide and surrounded by a field of black stubble. We still cannot see his eyes.

'Good evening, Mr Bright,' he says gruffly to Dad. How does he know his name?

'Hello?' says Dad, trying to hide his nervousness.

'Have you been for a drive? It's a nice night for it.'

'Um...' says Dad.

Moz steps forward and says, 'Yes we have actually. It WAS a nice night for it, before you turned up.'

The man looks angrily at Moz. He picks him up by his sweatshirt so that his legs are dangling and tosses him aside and onto the ground.

Then he steps over Moz and approaches Dad. He is standing so close to us now that I can smell him. He smells of old sweat, dank leather and cigarettes. Yuk.

Suddenly Dad notices something and says quietly, 'Harvey, is that you?'

The man doesn't miss a beat but replies in a much softer voice (almost as if he doesn't want his team of bullies to hear).

'Yes Stan, it's me. If you'd stuck around then maybe you'd be someone by now too. But instead...' Here he looks around at us in disbelief. He shrugs and then continues in the same menacing tone as before:

'Now, Mr Bright, I believe you were just about to tell me what you are doing here?'

'How did you find us?' says Dad, doing anything he can to distract him from our car.

The man sighs and says, 'You are a fool, Mr Bright. We passed your car on the motorway. That road is always empty and any car there is going to arouse our suspicions. We just typed your number

58

plate into our database and then...imagine our surprise when your name came out. Then it was just a case of following you from the service station up to here. You and your team of ...' Here he pauses and sniggers, 'tweens were pretty easy to track.'

Moz stands up tall and puffs his chest out to show he is not afraid. He is almost as tall as Dad, but still Harvey towers above him. 'Why are you so interested in Dad? We know you've been spying on him.'

My head is spinning and I jerk my brother's hand (which is still holding mine) and whisper, 'Is he from Conch?'

'Of course he's from Conch,' says John looking straight at the aggressive leather man.

Harvey's mouth puckers meanly. 'Obviously we're from Conch,' he says gesturing round at his silent colleagues. 'Mr Bright was one of our top employees before he got fired for his own stupidity.'

'Dad didn't want to work for Conch anyway. He says it's an evil company with no morals,' I say defiantly.

'Like I said, fired for his own stupidity.'

And then as I shiver, he bends his head down so that it is level with mine and only a centimetre away and breathes foul breath at me. 'So you've been testing your Dad's invention then?'

I nod my head. That is enough for him. He wrenches my hand away from my brother and holds my hand tightly with his big black glove. He pulls me towards him so that I am now standing next to him facing my brother and Dad. Alice, Dora and John are sheltering behind them.

'Now then, Mr Bright, are you ready to show us your car?'

Dad stares at him. Harvey looks from Dad to me and back to Dad. Dad nods his head in resignation. 'I'm ready,' he says.

--

Moz, Alice, Dora, John and I are standing over by the crates. Two of the men are standing with us. They have removed their helmets, revealing nondescript, sweaty heads. Close up, we can see that their leather jackets have a mini Conch logo on them. It is a pale silver conch shell on their right breast pocket. The men don't say anything, they just give us nasty looks now and again.

Dad has the bonnet of the car up and the remaining three men, including Harvey, the tall leader, are asking him questions. Dad is answering them quietly, giving away as little as possible. But it is difficult, they are poring greedily over all of my Dad's hard work, soaking it all in.

'It's not fair,' I say to John. 'He's worked so incredibly hard and those greedy men are just going to steal it.' John nods sadly.

'Are you ready to begin?' shouts Harvey at Dad.

Although Dad hates showing them the car he can't help himself getting a little bit carried away in the moment. He has spectators all around and he is preparing to amaze them.

'OK,' he calls, 'I'm ready. Do you want to get in?'

It is a funny sight watching three big men try and squeeze into our little car. Eventually two men are fitted in the back seat with their knees crunched up almost in their faces. Harvey is in the front seat. 'Best view,' Dad says to him and winks at us. He hasn't forgotten that when he starts the engine, the light will be almost blinding.

Dad prepares himself. He opens the driver-side door, ready for a quick leap in. Then he puts on his lead vest and protective helmet and visor. He holds the blowtorch in one hand and the matches in the other.

'Everyone ready?' he yells.

'Yes,' we all yell back, the men and us alike.

Dad lights the blowtorch. We leap behind the crates. Again, we hear a high whistling roar and the sky is filled with yellow light. The men beside us are crying, 'my eyes, my eyes.' It must be even worse for the men in the car as they were a lot closer to the blast. Dad has already thrown off the helmet and lead vest and jumps into the car slamming the door behind him. The car stutters off down the runway, slowly at first but gaining speed quickly and zooming off towards the other end at a great rate.

'Amazing,' says one of our guards, rubbing his sore, red eyes.

'Never seen anything like it before in my life,' replies the other.

Before we know it, the car has reached the end of the runway and is turning round with a screech of brakes. The bright beam of the headlights is burning down the runway towards us,closer and closer, brighter and brighter. The engine whines, it's going super fast. Dad steers slightly to his left, so he is pointing away from us; he doesn't want to hit us for a second time. Suddenly there is a yell, and Dad pounds on the brakes. He has carefully steered away from us but is heading directly into two of the motorbikes, left in the dark at the side of the runway. He is still going so fast that he has no control. He yanks the wheel round but it's too late he's hit the motorbikes with an almighty crunch. He's going so fast that the car piles over them, bursting all the tyres and pulling out the floor of the car from underneath the passengers. The car is still going and Dad can no longer steer or brake as the pedals have been torn out with the floor. The car is slower, but after bouncing over the bikes it is heading right for our crates. Again.

'Jump', yells Moz and we all run and dive away from the crates. With more of a dull thud than a crash, the car bumps and topples the crates before finally stopping.

10. BROKEN

We gather round the rather sorry-looking car. Dawn is just beginning and everything is coloured an eerie grey. Moz pulls open the driver door and Dad hobbles out. He has a nasty gash on his ankle from the crash, but otherwise he's fine. His passengers also look like they've escaped with only a few cuts and bruises. Harvey leaps out from the passenger seat and the two men that have been guarding us yank on the stuck back doors to let the back-seat passengers out. They look relieved to be free and unharmed. Harvey does a quick check that all his men are OK before lunging at Dad. Dad leaps back in alarm, but Harvey is playful and excited, not angry.

'Man, that was awesome,' he says, whacking Dad on the back in a congratulatory gesture. The other men gather round Dad too.

'Totally crazy. Well done, mate.'

'Astounding.'

'I wouldn't have believed it if I hadn't seen it with my own eyes.'

But Dad doesn't seem to be enjoying the praise. His head has drooped down and he says nothing. I think he has realised that there is no going back now and these men from Conch are going to take his invention away from him.

Sure enough, a minute later Harvey shouts to one of his men, 'Get on the radio, we need to get this car back to base. I reckon we can get it on the back of the tanker. Can you get someone to drive it up here on the double?'

The man pulls a two-way radio from his jacket pocket and I hear crackling and muffled voices. 'Ten minutes, Guv,' he shouts.

--

We all look at the car. It is in a very sorry state. The front and one of the sides are very bashed up. Trailing behind the car is the remains of the floor. The metal is ripped up and the exhaust is only hanging on by a thread. The tyres are torn up and three out of four of the hub caps have rolled away.

Two of the men go and examine their bikes. They have been practically flattened and are definitely never going to be ridden again. 'We'll need a lift back home,' one of them says, sighing.

'No big deal,' replies Harvey, 'we've got what we need,' gesturing towards the sorry wreck of the car.

Dad walks away from the car, he can't bear to look at it any longer. 'What now?' he says to the boss man. The men gather round Dad and they all start to talk together in slightly hushed voices.

Meanwhile, a little gleam has appeared in Moz's eyes. 'Go and try and listen to what they're up to,' he says to me, Alice and Dora. 'John, can you stay here with me?'

We wander over to where Dad and the men have gathered. Dad is spluttering with anger. 'We can't just leave them here alone,' he says.

'What's going on Dad?' I say, going straight over to him. He puts his arm protectively round my shoulder.

'They would like me to go with them,' Dad sighs.

'That is not for discussion,' says the tall brutish Harvey. 'You're coming with us. We need you to work the car. We need your brain. The only thing we have to decide is what to do with you, tiddlers? I vote we leave you here.'

'Never,' says Dad.

'Oh, be sensible please,' Harvey says exasperatedly. 'If we take them with us, what will we do with them? We don't want them hanging round Conch HQ causing problems. Besides we don't have enough room to take them all back with us.'

Harvey walks over to Alice and Dora. He puts a hand on each of their arms and holds them a little bit too tight. 'Now, girls,' he says, 'I'm sure you can find your way home, can't you?' They nod. 'And obviously you are much too clever to go telling anyone about this, aren't you? I mean, not while we are taking such good care of Mr Bright for you.' Alice and Dora nod vigorously. 'You see, Mr Bright, they are quite sensible really.'

Alice looks at Dad. 'Mum will be so worried if we're not back. We'll go home straight away and we'll be safe. Don't worry about us.'

Dad shakes his head. 'Is that the only way?'

We all nod. 'Yes, Dad,' I say and I give him a big hug. As I'm hugging him, I manage to whisper quickly in his ear, 'and we'll rescue you too!'

--

Only a few more minutes pass before we hear the rumbling of a heavy vehicle approaching. We see lights in the dawn sky and with a wrenching sound the tanker crashes through the wire fence at full speed. It grinds to a halt just metres from us all.

A man jumps out of the driver's side.

'Sub-agent Poopy reporting for duty, Sir,' he says, saluting Harvey.

'Poopy, we need to get that car back to HQ,' Harvey says. 'Can you rig it up onto the back of your tanker so we can tow it back?'

Poopy looks at the very battered old car and wonders why on earth they would want that pile of junk. But he does what he's told. With the help of some of the other goons, he has soon hitched the front of the car onto the back of the tanker and secured it with ropes. The back wheels drag on the ground. He tears off the broken floor that hangs behind the car and just in case anybody should want it, he throws it in the driver's seat of the car. 'Ready,' he calls.

Harvey inspects his work, 'OK, Poopy, back to base for you. Drive slowly and carefully, though. You have precious cargo.'

Poopy salutes and drives off again through the gap in the fence.

As soon as the tanker has rumbled off, he shouts, 'Right, men. Let's be off before it gets too light. Time to go, Mr Bright, you're with me.'

His team argue a little about who should ride on each bike. The two men whose bikes have been squashed are looking rather sad. No one wants to ride on the back.

Dad looks tired, exhausted and like he's about to give up. 'Are you sure you'll be OK, kids? Go straight home, please. Tell your mother enough, but try not to worry her too much.'

Alice takes control. 'Don't worry, Dad, we'll be fine. We'll go straight home. We're more worried about you, Dad. What will they do with you?'

'Look, kids,' Dad bends down and starts to whisper. 'As soon as I get to Conch HQ, they'll set me to work on the car. They know that they need me so much, because without me they've got nothing. They're not going to let anything happen to me. I'll probably be treated like a king: good food, all the equipment I need. No more messing about in the shed for me, so stop your worrying.'

Three motorbike engines roar into life, breaking the stillness of the dawn. Harvey rides up to us. 'Hop on, Mr Bright,' he says, gesturing to the back of his bike. Dad does as he's told and then looks at us with a sad but determined face. 'See you soon, kids.'

Harvey gives us a wave and a toot on his horn before all three bikes roar off down towards the motorway.

--

Dad has gone. The men have gone. The car has gone. All I can think about is Dad and his brilliant invention. And now both of them have disappeared off to who knows where. I try to stop myself, but I know I am going to start to cry. One tear rolls out and I try and sniff it back in, and then a whole lot more start to follow it. I am a big, brave, smart girl and I just can't stop crying. Alice must have heard me and she and Dora come up and put their arms around me. They look close to tears themselves. We stand together feeling utterly forlorn and at a loss what to do next.

It's Dora who notices first that the boys are not looking lost with us. In fact, they are nowhere to be seen. 'John, Moz, where are you?' she calls.

Two very cheeky faces pop up from behind one of the crates that have been scattered after their run-in with Dad's car.

'Crikey, girls, talk about feeling sorry for yourselves. Come and look at what we've got.'

We go over and have a look. Behind one of the crates is a big black cube with wires coming off it.

'What is it?' says Dora.

I fall back in surprise and land with a bump on another crate.

68

'My word,' I say, 'It's the engine, the nuclear fuel cell!'

'Yep,' says Moz, 'they've got our crumby old car and we've got the most super cool invention of the century. We win.'

11. A SPOT OF HARD WORK

'How did you manage it?' Alice asks Moz.

'Simple,' answers Moz, 'when Harvey and Dad were arguing about what to do with all of us, we just undid the screws that held the engine in the car and lifted it out. It's very heavy though.'

'I guess Harvey and his goons didn't realise that it wasn't the car that was valuable. Your Dad invented the engine, not the car,' adds John.

'Now we do have a bit of a problem, though,' admits Moz.

'Uh oh,' says Alice.

'We've got to get this very heavy and precious box home. And we no longer have a car to put it in.'

'Oh,' I groan. I suddenly feel very tired. I want to go home and go to bed, but somehow we still need to get the most important invention in the world back to our house. Why couldn't Dad have invented something small and light instead?

We start looking around in all the crates, trying rather half-heartedly to find something useful. The crates, however, are all either empty or filled with old and useless junk. Alice finds the last of the food from our midnight feast – we get half a Mars bar and 3 mint polos each.

At last John shouts from somewhere near the terminal building, 'I think I've got what we need.'

As he comes towards us, I see he is pulling a large luggage trolley.

'That's perfect, John,' I say excitedly, feeling more than a bit guilty for just sitting around feeling tired and desperate.

The trolley is newish and has four good, strong wheels and a big metal handle. John and Moz heave the box onto the trolley and we tie it on tight with some rope – at least we found plenty of that in the crates.

'Ready to be a dog-sled team again?' Moz asks with a laugh.

'You bet,' I reply enthusiastically. Dad's idea didn't seem that crazy at all anymore, in fact it seems to be the most sensible way to travel. We set up the bikes in a triangle formation again and soon enough Moz is again leading the way as we set off for the long ride back home.

--

The journey takes a long time. The trolley is heavy and hard to steer. Every time we reach a corner we have to stop and pull the trolley round, rather than risk it going off in the wrong direction to the bikes. Luckily there are no surprise vehicles this time and when we make it to our turning off the motorway, we still haven't seen a soul. The slip road up the hill to the roundabout is almost enough to finish us off. And when we almost lose control of the trolley on the roundabout, I almost wish that we'd never set eyes on the stupid engine. But even though we are all so, so tired now, we manage to make it back into town. There are a few more people around now, just people going off to work on their bikes or scooters.

'Just pretend what we're doing is completely normal,' says Moz, over his shoulder.

'I just hope we don't see anyone we know,' murmurs Alice.

We reach our house at last, ready to drop. We pull the nuclear engine into the house and leave it in the hall. It's just before seven in the morning and the house is still quiet.

'Mum must still be asleep,' I whisper.

'Let's go to bed,' says Alice, 'Mum probably won't even realise we've been out.'

We are all too tired to speak, let alone argue, so we all crawl off to our own beds and completely crash out.

--

My alarm clock says 2.07pm when I finally wake up. I feel a lot better, though. My stomach is very rumbly, so I head off downstairs to find some breakfast – or whatever meal you're supposed to eat when you start your day at 2 o'clock in the afternoon. Still in a daze, I almost trip over the engine, which is still in the hall. I smile to myself, glad that we've managed to keep Dad's invention safe. But that reminds me of Dad: he's not here. He's been kidnapped by horrible leather-clad men. What's Mum going to say?

But when I go into the kitchen, Mum isn't there. Moz and Alice are already up and Dora and John have come over already.

'Hey, honey,' says Alice, 'you sleep OK? Do you want some breakfast?' She is being overly motherly.

'Where's Mum?' I ask grumpily, sitting down at the table.

'She went to work,' says Alice and she hands me some juice and some scrambled eggs on toast just like I like them. I take them greedily and ungraciously. I really wish Mum was here.

'Mum left us a note,' says Moz. 'I don't think she's got any idea that anything's up.'

Hey you guys,

What's up with all my sleepy children this morning? I was all alone at breakfast. Dad must have gone out to his shed very early this morning because he was gone when I woke up. Oh well, hope you all have a lovely day in the garden and don't waste it all in bed. Eat anything in the fridge, look after yourselves and don't disturb your Dad in his work — he's very busy at the moment. Back at 6ish.

Love Mum

xxx

PS. Why's there a big battery in the hall? I want it gone by the time I get home.

'Oh dear,' I say, 'What are we going to tell her? She's going to be so worried.'

'It's so difficult,' says Alice, 'we'll just have to tell her the truth, I think.'

'I think maybe we'll have to hide some of it. She'll never let us out of the house otherwise, and we need to go and rescue Dad,' says Moz.

I shudder. I haven't really thought about that yet. Seeing Harvey again isn't top of my list of fun things to do.

'Anyway,' continues Moz, 'we've got all afternoon to think of a plan.'

--

I go into the office and start up the computer. Since losing my iPhone I've felt completely lost. I haven't spoken to my Facebook friends for ages. I go straight to Facebook and find loads of messages waiting for me.

Cherry> Yo Belle, whatcha been up to? (she's from California)
Bradley Jones> We've missed you. (he's from New Zealand)
Manoj Gopal> You've been missing for 2 whole days. We thought you'd forgotten about us. (he's from Mumbai, India)

I reply to them all:

Belle> Hey everyone. I've missed you too. You won't believe what's been happening here.
Bradley Jones> What? Tell me. Tell me.

I realise that it isn't safe to tell them everything, even though I really, really want to.

Belle> Um. Dad's had to go away suddenly. And my iPhone has been stolen.
Cherry> Stolen?
Belle> Well not exactly stolen. Oh it's all so complicated. Has anyone seen Fran the Spider?
Fran the Spider> Here I am.
Belle> I've got to go guys. I promise I'll give you a full update tomorrow.

I quickly close the group chat and start talking privately with Fran.

Belle> Oh Fran. I'm glad you're here.
Fran the Spider> What's up Belle? Did you lose your iPhone?
Belle> I didn't lose it. That guy Alec from The Gadget Shop took it in exchange for some information.
Fran the Spider> Really? Is he a spy?
Belle> Maybe he WAS one. Not a very good one I think. He just works in a shop now. But that's not all, Fran.

I try to tell Fran as quickly as I can about everything that's been happening. I tell him about the men from Conch and Dad inventing something that they really want. Finally I tell him about how Dad has been kidnapped and taken to Conch headquarters and that we have to rescue him but have no idea how.

> **Fran the Spider>** What can I do to help?
> **Belle>** I'm not sure actually. But it was good to tell you about it.
> **Fran the Spider>** Hey I'm always here.
> **Belle>** Thanks.

I close the chat window, feeling completely clueless about what I'm supposed to do next. I hope I've done the right thing trusting Fran.

--

John and Moz are in the hall staring at the fuel cell.

'Hi Belle,' says Moz. 'What are we going to do with this?'

'Put it in the shed?'

'But we don't have a key.'

'I know where Dad keeps a spare one.'

'But how do we get it there? It's very heavy, remember?' asks John.

'On the trolley from last night, silly.'

Moz and John nod in agreement and I skip outside the front door to find the trolley standing on the drive, just where we left it from last night.

It doesn't take us long to heave the fuel cell onto the trolley again and secure it with the same bits of rope. We start to drag it by its big metal handle. We squeeze it through the side gate and slowly start to weave through the fruit and vegetable beds towards the shed. As we get near the tall pea plants, Alice and Dora jump out in front of us.

'Ssssh,' they whisper forcefully, 'there's somebody in the shed!'

12. SPIES LIKE US

Moz doesn't waste a moment. 'Belle, do you still have the key to the shed?'

I hold out my hand with the key in it. He grabs it and gestures for us to follow him. Moz runs up to the shed and shuts and firmly locks the door from the outside.

'Who's there?' cries a voice in alarm from inside.

We go to the shed window. It is dusty and covered with cobwebs. We peer inside. A man comes over to the window, relieved, I think, to see that it's just us, no one more sinister. He looks familiar. He's short and fat and is wearing red baseball boots.

'Bob?' I mouth at him in surprise through the window.

'Yes,' he smiles, 'I'm a friend of your dad. Let me out and we'll talk. I'm on your side. I promise.'

We look at each other. 'Go on,' I say to Moz. 'Let him out. I think we can trust him.' Moz doesn't look totally convinced, but he goes to the door and unlocks it. We all stand behind him as he opens the door a few centimetres. 'Prove that you're a friend of Dad's,' demands Moz. 'We saw you here yesterday and you didn't seem that friendly then.'

Bob smiles and relaxes a little. 'That's easy,' he says, and gets out his iPhone. He quickly presses a few buttons and brings up a gallery of photos. 'Here you go,' he says and passes the phone to me. The first picture I see is one of Dad and Bob standing together, smiling. Dad looks a lot younger. He has lots of hair and isn't wearing any glasses. They are both wearing Conch jackets.

'Oh. Did you work at Conch too?' I ask.

'Yes. A long time ago. I left a few years before your dad.'

He takes the phone off me and scrolls through a few more pictures before reaching another one to show us. 'Look at this one too.'

In this photo, there is Mum, Dad, two young children and Bob. Bob is holding a newborn baby.

'Do you know Mum, too?'

'Yes. I've been friends with your parents for years. I just haven't been around much lately. If I had I might have had a chance to get to know you guys better. Can you guess who the children are?'

We all look more carefully at the children. I've seen pictures like that before, in fact, there's one that's ever so similar on our mantelpiece.

'That's me, isn't it?' asks Alice.

'Yes, and that's you, Moz.' he says, pointing to the little boy. 'And you, Isabelle, are only two days old in this picture.' I have a scrunched-up, pink face, poking out from many layers of blankets.

--

Five minutes later, we are all lounging on our lawn, chatting to Bob like we have known him for years (which I suppose we have). Bob brings us back to reality with a bump.

'Right then, I need to know exactly what's been going on here. Where's your Dad?'

Between us all, we manage to tell him everything that's been going on. He looks at the fuel cell, which is still in the garden, half hidden behind the overgrown potatoes.

'So this is it?' he asks, looking at the rather ordinary battery. 'This can power a car?'

'Yes,' says Moz. 'It can go really fast too.'

'He needs to do a bit of work on the steering though,' adds Alice, laughing.

The next thing Bob wants to look at is the satellite on the roof of the shed. I point it out. Bob is quite a fat, round man, but despite this he manages to crawl up the side of the shed with ease. With a sharp tug, he wrenches the satellite off the roof. Then he jumps down, catlike, and lands on all fours.

'Wow, I wish I could do that,' I say to Moz, thinking of our own rather clumsy attempts to reach the same thing.

'Me too,' he agrees, 'I wonder where he learnt to do that?'

Bob has brought the satellite down for us to look at. It still looks in perfect condition, a cold silver metal half-ball, bleeping gently to itself.

'So,' begins Bob, 'can you show me the website where you found the satellite for sale?' He has pulled a small laptop from his bag. It is the thinnest, lightest computer I've ever seen. As he opens the computer up, the screen saver pops up and the words "This computer is SLUmbering" dance merrily around the screen. He clicks off the screen saver into a web browser and hands it to Moz. Moz looks at it a second, 'I can't remember,' he sighs. I take the computer from him; this kind of thing is easy for me. I type in the name of the website www.sdotldotu.com and search for mini satellite 105. The picture of our satellite pops up straight away. I hand the computer back to Bob.

'Ah. This website, the very best. But I haven't bought anything from the spy gadget catalogue in ages. In my days at Spy Academy, training to be a spy, I'd always buy my gadgets from here. They sold everything a trainee spy could need, at a very reasonable price.'

So he is a spy. And he went to Spy Academy. I've never heard of Spy Academy before, but I suppose they wouldn't advertise it, would they? I wonder if that's where he learnt to climb like a cat?

'Are you a spy then?' I ask Bob shyly.

He smiles at me, 'Yes, I am. I did my training at the academy after I left Conch. I've been working as a freelance spy ever since.' I look a bit confused so he continues, 'Freelance just means I don't work for anyone in particular. I am my own boss. I work on my own gathering information and then I sell it. For the right price, of course.'

'But how do you know who's good and who's bad?' I ask.

'Well, Isabelle,' he says with a shrug, 'not everything is black and white. Some things are a little bit grey. We are all a little bit grey.'

I am worried by this. 'But we trusted you…'

'I know, Isabelle and I will repay your trust, I promise. I'm just saying that the lines between good and evil are a bit blurred sometimes. But I use my judgement and I don't sell information to someone who I know is going to use it for evil purposes. I am on your side. I'm just saying that I need to follow my own rules.'

'What about Conch?' asks Dora.

'Oh I would never give anything to them. They are deplorable.'

'But they've got Dad,' I cry, 'and if they are as bad as you say they are, we're never going to get him back.'

'We'll do it. We'll get your dad back,' says John. 'With or without Bob.' He gave Bob his best steely glare.

Bob stands up, 'No, kids. I'm going to do this one on my own. What if something happened to you? Your mum and dad would never forgive me.'

I stand up. 'He's our dad. I said we would rescue him and we will.' Moz stands up beside me and then John does too. We glare. Bob glares. No one says anything.

--

I'm beginning to wonder who will break the air of tension first. In the end, it is Alice who disrupts the silence,

'Bob, this website, the one that sells all the gadgets. What's it called? The guy in the shop said we weren't saying it right. He said it was some kind of code.'

We'd all forgotten about that and it's enough for me to put our disagreement with Bob aside, at least for the moment.

'Oh yes, I know,' says Bob, his easy smile coming back.

'I'm sure you can work it out for yourselves, if I point you in the right direction.'

Bob picks up his netbook and types the word SDOTLDOTU in big letters onto a blank screen. It looks like a nonsense word; I'm not even sure how you say it.

'Now can you see any real words in there?' prompts Bob.

'DO?' asks John

'Close, look again.'

'DOT?' asks Moz

'Yes,' says Bob, 'and?'

Suddenly something becomes very obvious to me and I prise the computer from Bob's hands. 'Tada,' I shout as I type S.L.U. into the computer. 'It says that doesn't it?'

'Yes it does.'

'Oh,' I say, suddenly deflated, 'but I don't know what that means either.'

'That's OK,' says Bob with a big grin, 'I'll tell you, but it's a secret, understand?'

We all nod excitedly.

'Spies Like Us. That's what S.L.U stands for, Spies Like Us. It's a group or community of spies. We use the code SLU to identify each other.'

'We use the SLU website to talk to each other, send each other messages. It's like a top secret Facebook.'

'But how do you know who's a good spy or a bad spy?' I ask.

'That's the same question you asked before, Belle. You don't. You just get very good at knowing who your friends are.'

I nod. I am beginning to understand.

'Now, think about it, kids. Have you seen the letters SLU together like that before, perhaps hidden in a word or in small letters? '

'Yes,' I gasp, 'just now on your screen saver it said "This computer is SLUmbering.'

'Great,' says Bob, 'I put that on my screen saver so that other SLU spies know I'm one of them. Anywhere else?'

We are silent for a minute, racking our brains.

'I know,' says Alice suddenly, 'there was one on Alec's badge in The Gadget Shop, it said "SLUrp" or something, I remember it made me wonder what he was slurping. Lemonade?'

'Excellent,' says Bob. 'Yes, he's definitely a member as he looks after the website. I wouldn't trust him, though. You remember what I was saying about spies not being black or white, well he's very grey. I wouldn't trust him at all.'

'Ooh! I know another one,' shouts Dora excitedly. 'I thought it was the strangest thing ever. Do you remember that man in the raincoat who got hit by the old lady on the bike? You know the one with the fake arms?'

We nod.

'Well he was wearing a little pin badge that said "I love SLUgs" and had a picture of a slug on it.

'That sounds like Crazy Jake,' says Bob sadly, 'he used to be the best spy ever.'

--

Just then Mum walks out into the garden.

'Here you all are,' she calls cheerfully. She stops suddenly.

'Bob?' she cries, 'Is that you?'

He jumps up. 'It certainly is,' he says and goes over and gives her a big bear hug.

'Bob, what's taken you so long? We haven't seen you in years.'

'I know. I know.'

'Hey Mum, I've missed you,' I say.

'Wow. You'd think I'd been to the moon from this greeting, not to boring old work. What's got into you?'

Moz sighs, 'Mum, we've got some bad news for you.'

Bob interrupts, 'Let me tell your Mum everything she needs to know. Laverne, I think you should come with me and have a quiet chat in the kitchen.'

Bob gently pushes Mum back towards the kitchen. When they are inside he firmly closes the door and we see them sit down together at the kitchen table.

'This is ridiculous,' says Moz. 'We should be talking to Mum. Not Bob. And I still don't trust him.'

'Well,' says Alice sensibly, 'we weren't sure what to tell Mum, maybe he can do a better job of it than us? She IS a worrier, so we can't just tell her that Dad has been kidnapped, she'll totally freak out.'

'And,' Dora adds, 'if he chooses not to tell the whole truth then we don't have to lie to your mum. I wasn't looking forward to that.'

I nod in agreement. There's no way I could tell even a half truth to Mum and I doubt Moz or Alice could either. She has a way of getting the truth out of us anyway. 'Why don't we go and listen at the window? I need to know what he's saying.'

We creep up to the side of the kitchen and slink down low so that we are just below the open window. Mum and Bob's voices float clearly out in the early evening air.

'So you mean Stan isn't here? He's not in the shed?' says Mum in a high-pitched panicky voice.

Bob's voice, smooth and calm, answers, 'That's right. He left late last night. But there's no need to panic. It's his invention. He needed Conch's expertise in the end. But they insisted on secrecy.'

'But he detests Conch Oil and all that it stands for. They'd be the last people he'd turn to.'

'Well, Laverne, it appears that in the end, he didn't have much choice and they forced him to go with them.'

'So,' and here Mum's voice was almost a wail, 'they kidnapped him?'

'No. No. No. They needed him, but they're not going to let anything happen to him. He's their star talent, always has been. When they've found out everything about the invention then they'll let him come home.'

'Oh. His invention. He'll be broken if they take that off him.'

'He'll find something new to do. But he'll be home soon, just like normal. Nothing to worry about.'

Moz whispers to me, 'Is he actually going to rescue him? It doesn't sound like it. Maybe he's more chicken than we thought.'

I reply, 'We'll go though, won't we? I'm not leaving him there.'

'Yes. We'll go tomorrow. And we won't let Bob or Mum get in the way.'

Bob must have heard the mumble of our voices under the kitchen window, 'OK, you guys, you can come in now.'

Bob insists on treating us all to take-away pizza. It's nice, but we all feel the empty space where Dad should be. Mum is surprisingly calm and seems convinced that if we all just carry on as normal, Dad will be back home in a few days. I think that perhaps Bob has done too good a job persuading her that there is nothing to worry about.

After dinner, Bob says that he must be off. 'Please stay,' says Mum, 'you've only just got here. There's not much room, but you are welcome to share a room with Moz. Keep us all company.'

Moz grunts his approval rather grudgingly.

'Alright, Laverne, that would be lovely,' agrees Bob.

--

Much, much later in the middle of the night, Moz shakes me frantically awake, 'Isabelle, Isabelle.'

'What?' I mumble.

'Bob's gone. His bed's empty. And I'm worried. We forgot about Dad's fuel cell. We left it in the garden.'

I am wide awake immediately. As quickly and quietly as we can, we make our way downstairs and out into the garden. The grass is wet and dewy under our bare feet. Moz swings his torch back and forth across the garden, 'Can you remember where we left it?'

'By the potatoes.'

We find the trolley by the potatoes, just as we left it. But our worst fears are true. The trolley is empty, the fuel cell has gone.

13. THE NON-PLAN

After a sleepless night, Moz and I join Mum and Alice for breakfast. Were we right to trust Bob? He's definitely nowhere to be seen this morning. Where's he gone? And how could we be so stupid as to leave Dad's invention just out there on the grass for anyone to take? Has Bob got it? It certainly seems likely. Is he off to sell it to the highest bidder? He is a spy after all. And you should never trust a spy.

Mum, however, doesn't seem that worried by Bob's disappearance. She says he's always been like that and he'll be back when we least expect him. Mum isn't sure whether she should go to work today, but Moz and Alice are insistent, 'What will you do, Mum, if you stay here? You'll just sit around worrying. We'll phone you if there's any news.'

Mum is finally persuaded to go to work and she heads out the front door. As she leaves, she almost trips over something on the front doorstep. 'Oh, Isabelle,' she calls back, 'there's a parcel here for you. See you all later. Byeeee.'

A parcel for me? I'm not expecting anything. Alice looks at me quizzically and I just shrug my shoulders, 'Lets go and look.'

I pick up the package from the doorstep. Dora and John arrive. 'Morning,' they chant gaily, 'What's that?'

'No idea. But come inside and I'll open it up.'

Everyone is intrigued by my parcel and we all gather round the kitchen table as I pull open the thick padded envelope. On the top of the contents is a note,

Dear Isabelle,

Alec here, from The Gadget Shop. I must apologise for any rudeness on my part when you visited the shop. If I had realised that you had such important friends, then of course I would have treated you with far more respect. Enclosed in this parcel is a brand new iPhone and some other things that "Fran The Spider" requested on your behalf.

I am very sorry.

Kind SLUrpiness,

Alec

My iPhone. Hooray. But what has Fran been up to? I pick up the smart new iPhone and give it a little shake to start. Immediately it starts to ring, Fran the Spider calling. The handset icon appears as well as a new icon for Facetime. Facetime allows you to see someone when you speak to them. Oooh. My old phone never had Facetime. I click Facetime and the screen flicks to an image of a tall lanky boy. He looks like he's about eleven, just like me.

'Who's that?' asks John.

'I think… Fran is that you? I'm Belle.'

'Hi, Belle, nice to finally see you at last. Yes, it's Fran here. Do you like your new iPhone?'

'It's fab, Fran. How did you get it?'

'Well, I cracked the S.L.U code.'

'Me too.'

'And then I just went onto the Spies Like Us website and got chatting to your friend Alec. I thought he deserved to be taught a lesson after what he did to you. I used video footage of a very dubious-looking man and pretended to be him while I talked to Alec. Like this...'

At that moment, Fran's face on the iPhone dissolves and is replaced by the face of one of the ugliest, meanest men I've ever seen.

'Urrgh,' says Alice, looking over my shoulder.

'Hi Alice,' says the ugly man from the iPhone, now with a huge grin on his face. 'It's still me, Fran.'

And then the picture fades back to my friend. 'I'm back. But I think I scared your friend Alec.'

'I think you really did.'

'Was there anything else in your package?'

'Ummm. I've got my iPhone back, thank you.'

'No problem. But there should have been something else as well.'

Moz, who has been standing behind me as well, reaches over to the almost empty envelope and tips it up. Out fall five credit cards, each with a cord attached. Each shows a holographic picture of the conch shell and the words "Conch Oil HQ" repeated over and over so that it covers the whole card.

'What are these?' says Moz, turning one of them over.

On the other side of the card is a photograph of Alice, and the words ACCESS ALL AREAS. When Moz turns over the other cards, he finds a photo of each of us. He hands them out and we hang them round our necks from the silvery cord.

'Are these what I think they are?' I say to Fran in the iPhone.

'Yep. Official passes to go anywhere in Conch HQ. Should help you find your Dad, I think.'

'They will. Oh thanks, Fran, these are so fantastic.'

'I wish I could come with you.'

'You can, sort of, I'll take my iPhone and I'll keep you up to date on everything that's happening. We might need your help again.'

'Super cool. Laterz.' And with that the screen fades to black and Fran the Spider has disappeared. For now.

--

'Right then,' says Moz, 'time for us to get going.'

'Going where?' ask Alice and Dora together.

'To rescue Dad, of course. We need to find Dad, rescue him and then get home before Mum finishes work!'

'Don't we need a plan?' I ask.

'What about food?' asks John.

Moz mutters something to himself about amateurs and then says, 'Belle, we'll just make up the plan as we go along. John, eat as much as you can now.'

John goes straight to our fridge and starts raiding it for food. 'Cold pizza anyone?'

Dora has a bigger concern. 'How do we get there? It's too far away to cycle.'

Dora is right. Conch built their smart new HQ and "office village" far outside the town back when everyone could afford to drive their cars.

'Ah', says Moz in a very superior fashion. 'I did some research last night and Conch has built a new electric tram line from the town up to their HQ, just so everyone can get to work. We can just hop on that. Any other questions?'

We are all quiet. And then, even though I don't like it and I've just had breakfast, I eat some cold pizza, just in case. It's going to be a long day.

14. CONCH HQ

We find the shiny new tram stop in the old bus station. A big sign declares, 'Trams every 10 mins to Conch Oil Village'.

'What's Conch Oil Village?' I ask.

'I think,' says Moz, 'that it's not really a village at all. It's just lots and lots of office blocks all in one place. Not everyone at Conch Oil works at the HQ, other people work in different offices nearby.'

'The funny thing,' adds Moz, 'is that all the offices and streets have really villagey names like "The Old Mill" or "Sunny Side Farm" so that it sounds like a village. But I bet it's all really ugly when we get there.'

We head towards the big metal turnstiles that lead onto the tram platform. 'Time to see if these passes actually work,' shouts Moz with a grin, his pass swinging round his neck.

Beside each turnstile is a scanner and we can see some business people showing their tickets to the scanner. Then they zip through the gates very quickly, before the gates slam shut behind them. Moz goes first and casually holds his pass up to the scanner. The ticket inspector watches with interest from a booth above the turnstiles. A green light pops up on the scanner and with a clunk and a click, the gate opens before him. He darts through and the gates close immediately. 'Your turn,' he beams at the rest of us. We all follow Moz's example and breeze through the gates.

As soon as we are through the turnstiles, Moz shouts 'Run, the tram's about to leave,' and we all dash down to the platform and jump on the tram just as the doors are closing.

The tram is pretty similar to a train. There are a series of carriages, but no engine or driver. It is all automatic. Each carriage has a big aerial on its roof to pick up its electricity from overhead wires. The big difference is that it can run on the now-deserted roads, rather than needing special tracks like trains do. The red LED sign at the end of the carriage tells us our destinations: 'The Old Dairy (offices A-J): 10 mins, 'Brown Cow Farm (offices L-Q): 12 mins, Big Green Field (HQ only and end of line): 15 mins'.

We quickly pass out of the town into the countryside. It is really very quiet and pleasant. How nice it would be if Conch Oil Village turned out to be a real village after all. The five of us don't talk much on the journey. We don't want to give ourselves away to the other passengers since the tram is crowded.

After a while the countryside begins to fade away and we begin to climb a steep hill. As the tram crawls up the hill, the trees and greenery become more and more patchy until we are left climbing a big empty concrete hill. As we reach the top of the hill, the 'village' opens up before us. There is a not a tree or anything green in sight. Everything is one colour: grey. There are streets and cul-de-sacs with wonderful sounding names like "Chicken Parade" and "Sunflower Street". But as we look down these streets, all we see are rows and rows of the same square concrete buildings.

We stop at the first tram station, "The Old Dairy," and some of the office workers get out and disappear into one or other of the identical office blocks. We stay on the tram. At every stop, more and more people get out; no one gets on. When we finally arrive at the tram's final destination, we are the only people on it. The last tram stop is called "Big Green Field," but sadly it's not green at all. As we get off the tram, we see a big grey field, made entirely of concrete, in front of us. In the middle of this is the tallest, greyest building of them all. A vast skyscraper towers above us and shining out from the middle of the building is the biggest conch shell I have ever seen. It's the logo of Conch Oil, a big silver-grey spiral shell and the words, "Welcome to Conch Oil Headquarters".

'We're here,' I say, shuddering at the sight of it. We stand together in front of the building.

'Do we have to go in there?' asks Alice nervously.

'Yes', I say, quietly but firmly. 'Dad's in there somewhere.'

--

We walk into the main foyer and take in our surroundings. The foyer is all shiny metal and big glass windows. It is also completely empty apart from a lonely-looking security guard in a small booth by the entrance. We all casually show our passes to him as we go in. He looks at them in a bored fashion and waves us in.

'Where now?' asks John, looking around puzzled.

I glance back at the security guard, but he has already gone back to reading his newspaper. The only route out of the foyer seems to be by lift. Thankfully, there are four of them at the back of the foyer and next to each is a list of what's on each floor.

'What a dull place to work,' says Alice as she starts to read out the list:

DEPARTMENT	**FLOOR(S)**
Administration	1 to 5
Finance	6 to 8
Human resources	9 to 10
Gym and Squash Court	11
Technical	12 to 17
Training	18 to 20
Administration for technical training	21 to 24
Junior and Middle Management	25 to 28
Very Senior Management	29
Security	30

'I've no idea where to start,' says Moz.

'No, I can't imagine Dad being anywhere like that,' I say.

'Well he must be somewhere,' says John.

'What about here?' says Alice, pointing at some small neat writing below the main list.

For NEW IDEAS LABORATORY, press 0 for basement. Special access required.

'That's it,' says Moz excitedly, 'he's bound to be there.' He presses the button to call the lift. The call light flashes and Moz presses the button again and again.

'But what about "Special access required"?' I ask.

'We'll be OK,' says Moz casually as the lift arrives and the doors swoosh open. 'Our passes say Access All Areas, remember.'

So we all dive into the lift and the doors close firmly behind us.

'Right then,' says Moz, glancing down the list of numbers and pressing 0, 'Here we go.'

But it's not alright, the lift does not move. It stays where it is. And then a recorded voice comes over a speaker from somewhere near the ceiling. The voice says, in a distorted inhuman kind of way, 'Special Access is required for the basement; do you have authority?'

'Yes,' says Moz a little hesitantly, 'we have passes.' He waves the pass in the air, in the direction that he thinks the voice might be coming from.

The voice seems unmoved. 'Please place your finger on the scanner.' From underneath the numbered buttons, a drawer glides out. The drawer contains a flat, finger-sized screen. 'Place your finger on the scanner,' the voice repeats, 'Access only for Conch employees. We have all fingerprints on file.'

'What do we do now?' I whisper, panicking, not sure whether the voice can hear us or not.

'I'm going to try it anyway,' says Moz as he places his finger on the scanner.

Immediately, a buzzer sounds and the automated voice says in a cross tone, 'Access denied. Access denied.'

A pause, what now? The lift judders into action, but it's going up, not down. The voice continues, 'The lift will now proceed to the 30th floor, where you can discuss your access arrangements with security officials.'

The lift speeds up as it gains momentum, we are passing the floors 10, 11,12…

John and I start pressing the buttons, any number between 12 and 30 will do. But the lift doesn't stop. 'This lift will proceed directly to the 30th floor. No stops allowed.'

The lift whizzes up through the floors… 27, 28. It starts to slow down… 29 and finally, 30. I grab Alice's hand as the door starts to open and she squeezes it back. Who will be waiting for us at the top?

--

Whatever we were expecting, it definitely wasn't this. Sunlight rushes in as the doors open. The top floor is all glass and is exceptionally bright after the artificial light in the lift. A man is waiting. He is wearing sports gear: shorts, trainers and a baseball cap. He is carrying a sports bag with some kind of racket sticking out. As he sees us, he gives us a soft smile and puts his finger to his lips. He calls back behind him to someone else on the top floor, 'It's fine, Scott, must have been a false alarm. No one's here.'

'OK, mate,' shouts back the other unseen man. 'You off duty now?'

'Yes, just off to play squash in my lunch hour, back soon,' our man replies, winking at us as he does so. And with that, he hops into the lift and the comforting dark of the lift returns.

'So…' says the man in a friendly tone, 'do you guys remember me?'

I look up at him puzzled. He does look slightly familiar. But it's Alice who works it out first, 'Poopy?' she says, still unsure. Poopy was the driver who towed Dad's old car away from the airport.

'That's right.' He grins again. 'How can I help?'

'Poopy,' I say, my mind all confused, 'why do you want to help us? You work for Conch, don't you?'

In answer, he just reaches up and gently taps his baseball cap. I look at his cap. It's one of those unremarkable American college ones. It says 'St Louis University' and has a picture of a baseball bat and ball embroidered on it.

'Did you go to St Louis University?' I ask, still muddled.

'No,' he answers, laughing a little, 'never even been to the States; I just liked the letters.' He pulls the cap off his head and muzzes his hair underneath, before throwing the cap down to me. St Louis University. S.L.U. Spies Like Us. Of course. He's a spy too!

'No time to waste. I believe you want to go the New Ideas Laboratory in the basement?'

We all nod. 'Yes, please,' says Moz. 'Thank you.'

'No problem,' he says and reaches into his sports bag and fumbles around. 'I know it's in here somewhere.' Finally he pulls out a thumb. It's a prosthetic thumb, not real, of course. 'Got this from our mutual friend, Alec, from the Gadget shop. The Spies Like Us website is still the best for reasonably priced spy gadgets.'

'How does it work?' I ask.

'Very simple. I've embedded my own thumbprint in it. The scanner will just think it's me. And as I'm security, I have special access to everywhere.'

Poopy then presses the 0 button and that annoying digital voice starts up again, 'Special access is required for the basement. Do you have authority?'

This time when the fingerprint scanner slides out, Poopy is ready for it and he presses the prosthetic thumb against the scanner. This time the digital voice says, 'Access granted. Proceeding to Level 0.'

The lift starts quickly this time and begins to descend rapidly to the basement.

'Now listen up,' Poopy says, as soon as the lift begins, 'we don't have much time. Do you remember Harvey?'

We nod. How could we forget that ogre, the leader of the goons who kidnapped Dad?

'Well, he's quite a big shot these days. Got some new invention that the bosses have got all excited about. He's become a very important person at Conch since you last saw him. Be careful. He's just as mean, maybe even meaner. But now he's super powerful as well. Watch out.'

'Thank you,' John and I say together.

He relaxes a little; his job is done. 'No problem, guys. I just hope I don't see you again. Here, you might need to keep this,' he says, thrusting the plastic thumb into my hand. 'Cheerio.' And then he presses button number 11, just in time, and the lift stops suddenly. 'I really am off to play squash, you know.' He leaps out, leaving us to continue rapidly to our destination.

15. HARVEY'S BIG IDEA

We are here at last:Level 0-The New Ideas Laboratory. It's where Dad is; I can feel it. The door of the lift opens. In front of us is a vast underground lab, far bigger than the skyscraper that sits above it. It's busy too. Hundreds of people whirl around us, engineers in their bright jackets, smart women in red lipstick and expensive shoes. All chatting excitedly, far too busy to even notice us.

The space is divided loosely into different areas by low moveable walls and in each area someone is demonstrating their idea. It's like a school open day or something. And indeed we realise that something special and unusual is going on. A poster on the wall advertises today's event:

NEW IDEAS FESTIVAL
EMPLOYEES ONLY.
COME AND SEE THE GREAT
NEW INVENTIONS CREATED
BY CONCH ENGINEERS.

Looking at the different booths, we see all sorts of different things being demonstrated. In one, a man in a pristine white overall is setting light to bright, coloured liquids in test tubes. We see one green liquid create a flame that leaps almost to the ceiling. There are "oohs" and "aaahs" from the audience; it's like a firework display.

In another booth, a man lies on a couch. He has wires stuck all over him, from his head down to each individual toe. He is surrounded by digital monitors going beep, beep, beeeeeeeep.

We walk on, following the crowds as they all seem to be drifting in the same direction. Suddenly John stops, his mouth gaping open in surprise. He has seen another poster for the festival, but this time it has a bright orange notice plastered across it:

HARVEY'S BIG INVENTION
3PM
DON'T MISS IT

Is that what everyone is going to see? What has he invented? I think I know what it is.

'I think I know what he's invented,' I say.

'You mean, what Dad's invented?' says Moz.

'Yes. It's Dad's nuclear car, isn't it?'

We all look at each other. 'What else can it be?' says John. 'He's not clever enough to actually invent something like this by himself.'

'He looked like he was about to steal it, even when we were still at the airport,' adds Dora.

Everyone is looking glum apart from Alice. 'Don't you get it, you guys? This means Dad is here. For sure now. Harvey couldn't be doing all this without his help. I want my dad back. Why should I care about some silly car?'

108

'Well it's not just a car. It's the greatest invention of the century...,' begins Moz, but then he tails off. 'But you're right. I want Dad back too. Who cares if Harvey takes all the credit?'

I smile and think of having Dad at home and sitting round the table, all of us talking at once. 'Let's go get him,' I say, leading the way to Harvey's show.

--

It's not hard to find. There are sign posts everywhere. 'Harvey's big idea,' say the signs with a big arrow pointing us in the right direction. Now everyone seems to be making their way there. There are crowds of people around us. There is a happy buzz, everyone glad to get some time off work, wondering if they are going to see something that will change the world.

We round a corner and see that this underground chamber is even bigger than we could have imagined. In front of us is a race track. A huge grand-prix style race course, the track curls off somewhere into the darkness. There are only two lanes and on the starting grid there are just two cars lined up. The first is an old-fashioned taxi, a black cab complete with its orange taxi light on top. The other I recognise. It's our car. Again. It's been fixed since I last saw it, but it still looks battered and old. There's going to be a race. Harvey is so proud of his new invention that he's going to demonstrate its power by beating an old-fashioned, petrol-burning car in a race. He's about to prove that the nuclear car is the future. No wonder everyone is so excited.

The noise of the people in this enclosed space is intense. We are squashed and pushed from all sides as people try and make their way to the barriers around the track. Someone is giving out flags to wave, 'Go Harvey!' they say. We are all gripping hands in a row; it's the only way to stay together in the crowd. Moz is at the front, dragging us through. He is pulling us towards a raised stand and seating area at the start and finish line of the race. All the big important people in suits seem to be there. They are making themselves comfy and almost rubbing their hands with glee. This invention could make Conch the most powerful company in the world. It would make each and every one of them millionaires.

Moz has pulled us underneath the stand where there is more space to breathe. He counts to make sure we haven't lost anyone. One. Two. Three. Four. Five. We're all still here.

--

We are trying to peer through the legs of the people on the stand. We can see the cars on the race track. It's difficult to see much, as more and more legs seem to be getting in our way. We can just see a group of men working round our car. They are wearing red overalls with the words TEAM HARVEY on the back. I'm pretty sure the biggest one is

Harvey himself and when he shouts obnoxiously at his team, 'Now. Now. NOW!', I know it's definitely him. Alice nudges me. She's looking at the man working next to him. He is shorter than Harvey and leaner too. He is wearing a baseball cap (also TEAM HARVEY) and glasses. He looks so familiar. And suddenly I know. I push my head between all the legs on the stand and start pulling myself through. I need to get closer. I ignore the little yelps of the ladies on the stand and a big gruff man who says, 'Hey you, stop that!' I'm through and I'm running down the stand, right up to the barrier. Just then the man in the glasses looks up in the direction of the stand and I know for sure. It's Dad.

I wave, trying to catch his attention. But Dad's not looking at me. He's looking beyond me with a concerned look on his face. I turn around and see something I really, really don't want to see. Just to the left of the stand I see four security guards, the men from the airport. Each guard has their hand clamped firmly on the shoulder of someone I know. They have all of them: Moz, Alice, Dora and John. I start to move towards them, calling out. Alice must have heard me and she turns towards me just a little and puts her finger to her mouth, 'Ssssh.'

I make my way as fast as I can through the crowds. As the men move through the people, the crowds clear away, making space for these nasty-looking men and their captives. I follow, but now I make sure I don't get too close. I can't let them get me now. As we move away from the racetrack, the crowds thin and I have to drop further back, diving behind the demonstration stands if anyone looks round. They reach the lifts quickly and all get in. I watch the lights on the lift as it starts to ascend. 1,2,3… all the way up to 30. They have gone to the security level on the top floor. I look around. The place is deserted. I have never felt so alone.

16. I HATE CCTV

I stand by myself, feeling utterly lost. I need a clue as to what to do next, but there's no one here to help. I know I need to be strong, but surely I can't do this by myself? If only there was someone to help me.

Now that it's so quiet, I notice something. It's something that's been going on for ages, but I've been too busy to realise it. There is a faint electronic sound coming from deep within my pocket. I reach in. Something is vibrating. It's my iPhone. Of course, Fran. I pull the iPhone out of my pocket so fast I almost drop it. I press the Facetime button and there is Fran, my friend, staring back at me.

'Belle, where have you been? I've been trying to contact you for hours. I've been so worried.'

'Oh Fran, I forgot about you. It's been so frantic. But now I don't know what to do. I don't even think you can help.'

'Belle,' he says reassuringly, 'you wouldn't believe what I can do. I have the whole of the internet, remember? Tell me what's up.'

So I tell him everything as quickly as I possibly can.

'Don't worry,' he says as soon as I've finished, 'I'm sure we'll think of something.' The look on his face tells me that right now he doesn't have a clue what to do.

'So the men just came and took everyone away up to the security office? How did they know you were all here?'

'Dunno,' I shrug.

'I bet they have security cameras. You know, CCTV.'

I nod. This makes sense and as I look around I see one pointing directly down from the top of the lift.

'Well,' says Fran, 'I think they've probably been watching from up in their security tower. They'll have a CCTV control centre and they must have seen everyone on that.'

'Yes,' I say, 'and they would have recognised us. I think they were the same men from the airport.'

Fran has gone quiet for a moment. He is thinking. 'I have a plan,' he announces eventually.

'Grab a chair,' he directs, 'and put it under the security camera. Make sure they don't see you.'

I find a chair and pull it round so it is directly underneath the camera. Fran instructs me to stand on the chair under the CCTV camera and to point the iPhone outwards so that it has the same view as the CCTV. 'Just hold it like that,' he says, 'just a few more seconds.' I wait, my arm aching from being stretched above my head for so long. At last he says, 'Got it, now hang on a second.'

I look at the iPhone screen. It is blank for a couple of minutes, until at last Fran's face appears and he says, 'Now watch this…'

The screen of the iPhone fades to black and then the image of the room behind me appears, the now-empty stands of the festival. Suddenly into this picture a really ugly man appears, the same man who Fran used to scare Alec. The man looks even more fierce than before, if that's possible. The ugly man growls at the camera before going off and starting to trash all the displays in a terribly violent fashion. He knocks over all the test tubes, kicks at the couch and roars in anger.

'Now,' says Fran, 'when you're ready, hold the iPhone up so it's directly in front of the CCTV camera. You'll have to hold it there until you see the lift start to descend.'

I understand now. Fran wants the security guards to come down, so I can sneak up and hopefully rescue my friends.

'I'm ready,' I say, standing up on the chair and lifting the iPhone screen high above my head, in front of the CCTV camera.

I wait. Nothing happens. My arm aches. I lean back a little so I can see the lift lights. There is only one lift on the 30th floor at the moment. If this works, they'll come down in that. What if they haven't seen it? Then, at the moment that my arms feel like they might fall off, I see the lift start to move; the numbers quickly descending from 30 to 0.

'They're coming, Fran! They're coming,' I shout, pulling the iPhone down so I'm looking at the screen. I see the ugly man smashing stuff up for a second and then Fran reappears.

'No time to waste. Stand right next to the door. You want to jump in as soon as they come out. They won't be looking for you.'

'OK, thanks. Bye, Fran,' I say, about to hang up.

'Don't!' he cries, 'leave it on. If I'm in your pocket I should be able to hear most of what's going on. It was horrible being here and worrying about you all.'

'No problem,' I reply, shoving the iPhone into my pocket with Fran's face still looking out at my pocket lining. I wait by the door: 3,2,1,0. The doors open and the four men come rushing out. I dash straight in and press 30 as quick as I possibly can. The men have stopped a few metres from the door. They are confused as the ugly man is no longer there and are looking all around them. Just in time the doors start to close and the lift begins to climb. I know when I get there I won't have much time.

--

The lift ascends swiftly to the 30th floor. As the doors open, the bright sunlight makes me blink. There doesn't seem to be anyone here. Fran's brilliant plan has worked. I dash to a central room and look in, it's the CCTV control room. About fifty TVs are showing different things, all around the HQ building. One row of screens seems to be showing just the basement and I see the race track, heaving with people. I look at my watch, 2.45pm. I've got fifteen minutes to find and rescue everyone before the race begins. This is crazy. I can see the security guards on one of the screens. They are still there in the basement, but they are looking puzzled. Any minute now, they'll start heading back upstairs.

I look around the open-plan office; it seems empty. Where are they? I start to shout, 'Moz! John! Alice! Dora!' Immediately, I hear a loud banging coming from a cupboard. CLEANING EQUIP-MENT ONLY reads the sign on the door, 'Are you in there?' I call.

'Yes!' they shout.

I look at the door. There is no handle that turns, or a key, or keyhole. I push the door hard, but it doesn't move an inch. It doesn't even rattle.

I look to one side. There is a small card swipe machine. Could it be that simple? My pass still hangs round my neck and I nervously swipe it through the reader. A little green light comes on with a ping and the door swings open towards me. Everyone falls out: Moz, John, Dora, Alice and Bob. Bob! What's he doing here?

'Thank goodness you're here,' says Alice. 'That cupboard was too small and way too smelly.'

'Where now?' asks John.

'Run for the lift,' I shout, 'they'll be back any minute.'

We all run towards the lift, luckily one still sits open from when I came up. There is another lift on its way up, it's at 28,29… 'That's the men coming up,' I yell. We dash into our lift and just as Moz is reaching for the button 0, I stop him, 'No time to do all that finger print stuff now.' I press 29 and the lift doors begin to close.

--

We tumble out of the doors on floor 29. No one seems to be around. There are huge offices here, with big, squidgy armchairs chairs and lots of pot plants. It's very, very plush. The big bosses must work here, but luckily they're all downstairs watching the race. Bob recovers first and says to me, 'Well done, old girl, glad you're on my side.'

'Great job, Belle,' says Moz.

'No problem,' I say, feeling very proud of myself, 'But there's no time to waste. We've got to rescue Dad.'

'Um,' says Bob, 'I've got a bit of an extra problem.'

'What's that?' says Moz seriously.

'I'm a wanted man here. They caught me at the door. I'll be caught in minutes as soon as I move.'

'Maybe we should leave you here?' says Moz. Alice protests, but Moz continues, 'We don't owe him anything. It's Dad we came to rescue; Bob's just got in the way.'

Moz is right, sort of. Bob hasn't exactly done a good job of rescuing Dad so far. But then neither have we. In fact, I'm the only one who HASN'T been captured. I think of that photo of Bob, cradling me in his arms as a baby.

118

'No,' I say, 'Bob's coming with us.' I look at his tatty raincoat. 'And I know just how to do it.'

Bob's raincoat has reminded me of that mad old spy we saw on the road, the man who was hit by the bicycle. Anything can be hidden under one of those coats, maybe that's why spies like them so much? I ask John to put on the raincoat. He's not very keen. It's not exactly his style. Then I ask him to climb up and sit on Bob's shoulders. We button up the coat for them and Bob is hidden inside. It's not perfect; John looks very tall and is rather out of proportion being so skinny on top and fat on the bottom.

Moz laughs. 'If anyone asks, John, just say you're a pro-basketball player. They're all really tall. Are we ready?'

It's time to go and get Dad and go home. We climb back into the lift. John/Bob duck slightly to avoid bumping John's head. I get the prosthetic thumb out of my pocket. I press 0 on the lift, and we start to descend.

17. THE RACE

My watch says 2.59pm when the lift doors open on the underground level.

'Let's run,' I say, and we dash out of the lift and sprint to where the race is just about to start. The place is busier than ever. Everyone is focussed on the race and thronged at the barrier, waving flags and waiting for the excitement to begin.

We make our way behind the crowds until we reach the stand. There's still fifty or so people in front of us and we're desperate to see what's going on. 'Follow me,' calls Bob, muffled beneath the coat. The very tall John/Bob barges through the people in the rudest way possible. 'Out of my way,' shouts John. We follow behind them as close as possible before the crowds close behind us again. The people grumble and groan, but we squeeze through. We reach the front, and Bob rips open his coat, 'I can't breathe in there.' John jumps down and we sit on the edge of the barrier. We've made it just in time for the action.

The two cars are lined up on the starting grid. The shiny black cab, running on petrol and our ancient old car, running on who knows what.

'Dad's car isn't going to work is it?' asks Alice.

'What do you mean?' I say.

'The engine, the fuel cell, it's not here. We took it out, remember?'

'Do you think they've made another one?'

'In two days, no chance,' says Moz. 'I wonder what IS going to happen?'

The driver is already sitting in the petrol taxi, ready to go. Around our old car, Harvey and Dad are arguing. Dad must know that this is going to be a disaster, but does he care? Perhaps he wants it to go wrong. Dad is holding a blowtorch and has a helmet with a visor. He puts the visor down. Harvey puts on his dark glasses and gets in the driver's seat.

The tannoy crackles into action. 'Ladies and Gentlemen,' says a loud clear voice, echoing all over the underground track. 'Ladies and Gentlemen, the race is about to begin. For your safety, you must close your eyes as the race starts. There will be a bright, blinding light for a few seconds. Please close your eyes when I say Go. We will announce when it is safe to open your eyes. Is everyone ready?'

The crowds go wild with excitement. 'On your marks,' begins the voice.

'Get set.'

'Go.'

--

At this moment, the world seems paused. The crowd is quiet, eyes closed obediently. We, of course, have our eyes open. We know there's not going to be a blinding light now. The petrol car has chugged off round the track, but our car is still and silent.

'DAD!' we shout. Dad is standing over the lifeless car. When he hears our voices he raises his visor and blinks out at us. He can't believe his eyes. 'Dad,' we shout again. He chucks off his helmet and runs over to us, grabbing us all and holding us tight. 'That,' he says, pointing at our wreck of a car, 'is never going to work.'

'Let's get out of here,' says Moz.

'I can't,' says Bob, 'I'm a wanted man, remember?'

'Bob!' says Dad, seeing him for the first time, 'what are you doing here?'

'Rescuing you, of course.'

We glare at him and he changes his mind quickly. 'Actually, these guys are rescuing you. I'm just getting in the way. I didn't realise that I would still be a wanted man here, after all this time.'

'Well,' says Dad, 'you shouldn't have tried to blow up that oil tanker, should you?'

I'm shocked. 'Bob?'

'Yeah,' says Bob sheepishly, 'that's a grey area.'

'Here,' says Dad, pulling off his red overalls and cap and thrusting them at Bob. 'Put these on.'

--

Meanwhile, the crowd is getting restless and people have started to open their eyes. There is a

123

general murmur of confusion. Has it been a success? But then they see the car still sitting there on the starting line and they realise. We can feel the atmosphere in the room changing. Flags are lowered. People start to mumble and grumble. 'What a waste of time.' says one. 'He can't even get it started,' says another. The big bosses sitting on the stand behind us are even more cross. One man sits with his head in his hands. A second shakes his fist. A third says loudly to anyone who might be listening, 'I always said that Harvey wouldn't amount to anything. How right I was.'

At this point, Harvey is still sitting in his car. I don't think he can believe this is happening. He knows his big moment is ruined. He will be back doing security tomorrow. He looks round for Dad to share his humiliation. When he finally spots him, laughing over by the barrier with us, his face grows red with anger and he leaps out of the car. He slams the door behind him and it rattles and hangs off its hinges limply. As he storms towards us, I see that Dad is no longer afraid of him. And to my surprise, I am not either. Not one bit. We stand next to Dad, ready to face Harvey together. But we find that we don't need to. The crowd has seen Harvey and has started to boo. A few people at first and then the whole track echoes in one huge 'Boooooooooooooooo.' People are climbing over the barriers and going to see him directly. Soon there is a queue of people, bombarding him with questions and complaints.

'Come on,' calls John, 'lets make a run for it now. While everyone's busy.'

'Good idea,' says Dad and we start to head back through the already thinning crowd. I notice that Bob has disappeared. But I can't worry about that at the moment, we have much bigger problems. Standing all round the edge of the crowd now is a ring of security guards. A lot more now than there were before, maybe thirty or forty of them. They are all dressed the same, all in black with a peaked cap, labelled Security. Of course, they all work for Harvey. There's no way they're going to let us get away. They are letting the crowds leave, but they are checking everyone, watching and waiting for us.

Moz spots them first and pulls us all round back towards the stand. Too late, one of the security guards has seen us. He gestures to some of his mates. 'Over there,' he says and a gang of security guards begin to head in our direction. Moz turns to Dad, 'What do we do now?' he asks. Just then, one of the big bosses on the stand calls, 'Stan? Stan Bright? Is it really you? It is. Well. Howdy-doody. Good to see you, old man. What are you doing here?'

Dad looks up at him uncertainly. 'My old boss, Mr Trooper,' he whispers to us. The security guards have reached the edge of the stand. They are looking at us and then up at Mr Trooper uncertainly. This has at least bought us some time.

I lead the way up the stand. I want to get as far away from those security guards as possible. 'Hello,' I say politely, 'I'm Isabelle. I'm Stan's daughter.' I reach Mr Trooper and shake his hand.

He shakes my hand warmly, 'Well, hello, little girl. Charming to meet you.' He turns to Stan, 'So you've brought your delightful family to watch the show?'

'Yes,' says Dad, 'we heard about the great invention and I really wanted to see it. It could have been a historic day.'

'Yes, indeed,' says Mr Trooper, a little wistfully. 'It could have been a great day. Good to see you, though. Not thinking of coming back and joining good old Conch Oil?'

'Not at the moment,' says Dad politely.

Two smart and suited men join the conversation. 'Ah long time no see, Mr Bright, good to see you back. Are you sure we can't convince you to join us again?'

'No,' says Dad politely but firmly.

The second man, turns to Mr Trooper. 'What a mess,' he says. 'Thought it was too good to be true.' The men soon begin talking about Conch Oil, Dad joining in now and again. We are stuck here, listening to the men drone on. The security guards show no sign of leaving. Even more guards have arrived at either side of the stand. We are trapped.

Just then the taxi roars round the race track and screeches on its brakes at the starting line. A man in red TEAM HARVEY overalls jumps out and opens the doors. As he looks up at us, he raises his cap ever so slightly. Bob!

'Anyone need a lift?' he shouts.

18. A WHIFF OF PETROL

We run like the wind down the stand. The security guards follow us, but it's taken them valuable seconds to notice what's going on. The big bosses watch us run off in amusement.

'You'll be back, Stan,' they call after us.

'Not if I can help it,' shouts Dad, grinning as he runs.

We pile into the taxi. Dad in the front and the five of us all in the back. We slam the doors and Bob guns the engine.

'Where to?' says Bob as we zoom off down the race track.

'Home, please,' I shout above the noise of the motor. We look out the back window at the rapidly disappearing figures of the security guards. We wave goodbye.

'How are we going to get out?' I ask, remembering we are all underground. The track sweeps round in a circle ahead of us, if we follow it round we'll end up back at the starting line. We peer out of the windows into the gloom.

'Fire exit!' yells John, and Bob hauls the steering wheel round and we head in that direction. 'It's locked,' I say, looking at the tightly closed wooden doors. 'Not any more, it's not,' shouts Bob as he drives the taxi fast, straight at the doors. With a crash and a splinter, we are through, bombing down a thin, echoey tunnel. It's pitch dark here; the taxi's headlights are the only light.

'Where are we going?' asks Alice, from her position squashed in one corner of the back seat.

'No idea,' says Dad, 'but I hope this will take us outside eventually.'

The tunnel seems darker than ever as we twist and turn through its dank corners. Behind us a rumbling and suddenly more headlights, three to be exact. 'Motorbikes!' I say.

'Crikey,' says Bob, pressing harder on the accelerator.

As we turn yet another corner, the colour around us changes from black-black to ever so slightly grey-black. Daylight? It's definitely getting brighter as we continue on our way, but the motorbikes are getting closer.

Suddenly, we go round an extremely sharp bend and end up thrown into the middle of a street. A normal, outside kind of street.

'Where are we?' asks Dora.

'I think,' says Moz, 'yes, we're in Conch Oil Village. Look at the sign, we're on "Dandelion Drive".'

I look around us. We've come out of a small, nondescript entrance; there are offices in front of us and all the way down the cul-de-sac. To the right, however, is the end of the street and after that we can just see the start of the hill that leads the way out of the village. Bob instinctively turns towards the exit, trying to get away as fast as we can.

I think of the motorbikes, only seconds behind us. 'No,' I shout, leaning over to the driver's seat and almost pulling the wheel back round, 'go in there.' I point to the office building directly in front of us, "Office J" it says.

'What, in there?' questions Bob.

'Yes,' says Moz, getting my plan. 'Go straight in the doors.'

Bob follows our instructions and points the taxi at the large glass double doors ahead of us. As we approach, slowly now, the doors open automatically, and Bob eases the taxi in and through into the foyer. Bob switches off the engine and we hold our breath. A second later we hear the motorbike engines screaming out of the tunnel. The noise halts. 'They're looking around,' whispers Moz. A few agonising seconds later, we hear the engines roar again and then we hear the drone of the motorbikes get less and less until it finally disappears.

A knock on the taxi window startles us all. A smart young lady is at the driver's window. Bob winds down the window. 'They've gone,' she says as if this kind of thing happens all the time. 'Thanks!' we all say.

--

It's kind of fun driving home. It's a long time since I've been in a car. We wind down the windows and let the warm wind ruffle us. We have taken a detour off the main road to avoid any motorbikes. We are driving down small windy country lanes. The late afternoon sun makes the fields golden and homely. Occasionally we pass someone walking along. They stare at the very unusual sight of a taxi. We grin back and wave.

Dad turns round from the passenger seat, 'So kids, any idea where my fuel cell went? Harvey never realised it was missing, not until it was too late, of course. I have been pretending to work on thin air for the last two days. Did you take it? Did you take the nuclear engine at the airport? I can't think what else could have happened to it.'

'Well,' begins Alice.

'It's a long story, Dad,' I say. 'We did have it. But then we lost it. I'm really sorry Dad.' I glare at Bob, but he drives on, oblivious.

'Oh,' says Dad, disappointed. 'Oh well, it's all in here, I guess,' he adds, pointing at his head. 'But it will take a good few years to get back to the stage I was at.' He brightens up again, 'Hey, but horrible Harvey doesn't have it, does he? And I'm going home. Thanks to you guys.'

--

We are driving up our little road at last, almost home. Bob parks on our drive and crunches on the hand brake. Home. At last.

Mum must have heard the engine as we came up the road. She appears out of the house as soon as we stop. She watches us all climb out. When she has counted all five children plus her husband she gives the biggest smile ever, and we run over to her. 'Mum!'

'I don't know what you've been up to, but I am so so glad to see you. I've been worried sick.'

John and Dora's dad is there behind Mum. He's been at our house, worrying with Mum.

Bob appears out of the front seat. 'Not Bob too?' says Mum laughing. 'That really is everybody accounted for.' She gives Dad the biggest hug. Dad says, 'Bob came to help. But it was our kids, and Dora and John, of course, who saved the day. Honestly, Laverne, we should be so proud of them.'

'Well, I am, of course I am.' Mum smiles. She grabs my hand and holds it tight. 'Come on, everyone come in. The neighbours are wondering what on earth we're up to.'

Dad says, 'I'll be in in a sec, I'm just going to check on my shed.' He slopes off round the side of the house and into the garden. Mum tries half-heartedly to stop him. 'You'd better not be long!'

--

We are all sitting in the kitchen, wondering what's for tea when Dad comes bounding in.

'You'll never guess what I've just found!'

'What?'

'Only my fuel cell. I thought you said you'd lost it.'

'We did,' says Moz, 'we brought it all the way home from the airport. But we left it in the garden overnight and it disappeared. We thought Bob had stolen it, to be honest.'

'I stole it?! Never!' says Bob. 'I just put it in the shed for safe keeping.'

'I can't believe it,' says Dad, delighted, 'I can start work on it again tomorrow.' Mum sighs. 'Now all I need is a new car to test it in,' continues Dad.

'There's a taxi on our front drive. Why don't you just use that?' asks Alice.

Dad dances round excitedly, 'Of course, of course.'

Mum interrupts, 'With all this commotion, I haven't got anything for tea. Are you guys hungry?'

'Starving.'

'Oh well, pizza again?' she says, picking up the take-away pizza menu.

'Definitely,' we all agree.

--

Fifteen minutes later all of us: Mum, Dad, me, Moz, Alice plus John, Dora and their dad. And Bob, of course. All of us are squeezed round our kitchen table, enjoying our pizza.

'This is the life,' says Bob, raising his drink in the air. 'Cheers,' we all say.

'Before I forget,' I say, 'There's someone else we've got to thank.' I pull my iPhone out of my pocket and place it on the table.

'Everyone,' I say, 'this is Fran. He's from South Africa and he's been helping out every step of the way.' Fran is still on Facetime and his bewildered face stares up at the nine friendly faces looking down at him.

'Fran,' I say, 'these are my friends and family. Welcome.'

Everyone raises their glasses again. 'To Fran,' we cry.

After that messages from my other Facebook mates start to pop up on the iPhone.

'Hello,' one says.

'What's been going on?' says another.

I whisper, 'Bye Fran, talk tomorrow,' into the iPhone and switch it off. Not tonight. I'm too busy with my family and my real friends. I punch John playfully on the arm.

'Ouch,' he says.

Yep, he's definitely real.

THE END